The locations within this book
to actual persons living or dea
This book is a mix of fiction and lived experiences that have been blended together to create the society in which the story is set.

Donna, thank you

x

CHAPTERS

PROLOGUE

The year was 1987 and Andy Taylor from pop icons Duran Duran, released Thunder, his first solo album. This was never going to win awards but even now, 30 years or so later it is still sits within my top twenty records of all time. Why? Because it helped me through some tough, rough times as I was growing up.
Every morning I used to deliver newspapers, and all I had to keep me company was my Walkman and the Thunder LP. My Walkman wasn't great and had a tendency to chew the tapes up or play the music I was listening to slightly too fast, but over time I got used to the high tempo version of this 9-track masterpiece. Thinking back, I really enjoyed that hour I had to myself every day, and Thunder became my newspaper delivery soundtrack. But once that last paper got delivered, it was time to return home.

By now I was used to the beatings, the abuse, the bullying, the bruises. It had become somewhat the norm now. Even on the walk to and from school I had my fair share of scraps with the local Indian kids. So, did this violent upbringing make me street wise and physically intimidating? No, not in the slightest, but it provided me a different way of viewing the world. A way that not everyone would agree with.
I'm no longer concerned with the principles of right and wrong. I'm no longer worried if you agree with me or

not. Why? Because I've killed 13 people, and I have 13 more to go.

The man who abused me is dead. Sadly, not by my hand, but he's dead, and that is what's important. Actually no, that's wrong. What would be important would be the reason behind why he abused me? Did he take pleasure in beating me? Pleasure in using his belt or shoes to control me? Pleasure in rubbing my face in puddles of his piss? Pleasure in destroying my childhood?

The ultimate question I suppose would be how did he die? No, why did he die? Why! Answer my questions cunt. Answer them! But he never will.

I'm on my way back from Macclesfield where I killed a man. I use the term man very loosely as he and his associates were nothing but scum, yet this scum delivered to me a moment of absolute clarity. I now know who I am.

The guy sat opposite me on the train has no idea who I am, or what I've done. I'm just staring at him as he tries to avoid eye contact with me. His little fat face reflects on the train window and every time we go through a tunnel, I can see his eyes flick toward me then back again. Why is he so nervous? He looks tired. Weak. A man without a backbone. His suit is cheap and the gold band on his finger can no longer be removed as his body

has clearly expanded more than his wife had ever wished it to. He probably hasn't had meaningful sex in months.
I bet his workforce consists of nothing more than pale middle-aged women and a couple of his best mates who all no doubt lack the intelligence and ambition to move beyond his office.
Weakness. I hate weakness. It's the one trait in people that fucks me right off. Especially if those people are in a position of alleged power or authority. When dealing with people like this I always think back to a little ditty I composed some time ago.

THERE IS ONE THING IN THIS WORLD THAT'S TRUE AND THAT'S, I CAN'T SPELL CUNT WITHOUT U.

Apologies for the bad language but that is the way I talk. Sadly, I have met so many of these slimy, spineless bastards over the years and almost all of them in the workplace. Just like this ginger prick sat in front of me.
I can't help but smirk at him as he gets increasingly nervous, but just as I start to enjoy myself, he fucks off at Coventry. Shame, he was fun to look at.
I grab a drink out of my bag, put my headphones on and relax. Just a couple more hours and I'll be home.

THE FIRST ATTEMPT

This is where it all begins, in Andover. What a boring little place! Leaving the train station, there is nothing to look at apart from a taxi rank and a couple of bus stops. Where's the pub? I pick a direction and start walking. The direction I chose? Left, along Station Approach. The funeral place looks quiet, let's see if I can change that.

I carry on walking and end up on Junction Road. The next road is long, generic and boring, just house after house after house. All with what look like matching driveways and front doors. I can't walk down this road any longer. It looks like it will never end!
I need to scout these places before I visit or at least work out what is what online before arriving because this is ridiculous. Why didn't I pick Accrington, Ascot or Alton? At least at Alton there is Alton Towers, yet here I am in bastard Andover. Moving as quick as I can back to the station. I need to plan this properly if I want this to work.

ONE : ANDOVER

It has been just over a year since I visited Andover and during that time, I've been a busy little bee and actually have a plan. Not just any old plan, but a seriously fucking clever plan that I'm sure will have me listed as one of the greatest killers in the history of the UK. Finally, something to tell the grandkids about.
I have meticulously worked on every area of my upcoming adventure and have covered myself for every possible eventuality. Train tickets were all purchased well in advance from various places using various payment options, and I've even handed money to the homeless to buy me tickets in case CCTV operatives put two and two together somewhere down the line. Ticket Master, as I have dubbed him, is my main go-to guy for getting me what I need. His real name is Neil, but I do not like that name, so I renamed him. He doesn't mind; I pay him well.

I have spent a lot of time researching, planning, and spending lots of money. I have lots of money in case you were wondering. Roughly 3.2 million in the bank, or to be exact £3,284,361, and how I got that money? Maybe I'll share that with you another time. We are going to be spending a lot of time in each other's company I suppose, and train journeys can get a tad boring. Speaking of trains, here's mine.

Now you've probably gathered by now that I'm not a natural storyteller, nor am I a natural born killer, but people change. Apparently, leopards don't but I'm not a leopard. If I was an animal, I think I'd be a bird of some kind. Probably a crow, or a penguin. Maybe a city pigeon? You know the one with the leg missing or the weird curled up foot. The one you try to throw bread at but it's always too scared to go for it because it got beaten up once by a gang of obnoxious gulls. The one you'll find dead in a road, recognizable as nothing more than a pile of distorted feathers. Yeah, I'll be that bird. No one likes it, and it won't be missed when it's gone.
This train is quiet. I guess there isn't much demand to travel to Andover?
I wonder if there is an area in Andover called Under? Under Andover.

We've just changed at Basingstoke. I'll be back here soon, so I made sure I was well covered, and my face was unrecognisable. It's raining, so that helps. Hood up, umbrella open and collars pulled up. It's not cold out, but I don't look out of place as many others are doing their best to shelter from the rain. Basingstoke station is covered in most part, but I make sure I spend a couple of minutes in the rain, so my umbrella gets wet. No idea why? It just seems like the right thing to do.

I'll be getting off at Andover in about 5 minutes and I'm feeling like the butterflies in my stomach have got the shits.

I need to show composure. Relax and breathe. In for six seconds, hold for six seconds, then out for six seconds.

666 and repeat.

As we all start to do that shuffling around thing that we do a minute or so away from our destination, I spot a rather odd looking little man sat about 4 seats in front of me on the opposite side of the aisle. He's wearing a plain white t-shirt and baggy purple shorts. His head is the same size as his body and his arms are freakishly thin. He obviously doesn't feel the cold, and I would say he is going to be attracting attention. Quite the opposite to me really so I'm quite glad he's on here and getting off at my stop. Everyone will most certainly be looking at him and his massive head.

I leave the train and make my way out of the station. I know where I'm going, and I'll be doing this all on foot. As I've done with all 26 locations, I have gone online to scout the areas for CCTV coverage, traffic cameras and anything else that might record me. I know trains and train stations are covered by CCTV and that is why I have a large range of masks and disguises, but I will explain in more detail about those later as I'm hard pushed for time right now, and more than a little nervous. In fact, I feel sick and I think I'm going to shit myself.

I keep telling myself to be in the moment. Enjoy the

feeling. Enjoy the sense of panic and stress. These are authentic emotions and like relief and euphoria, they need to be fully explored and enjoyed.
I repeat this time and time again until I eventually accept my physical and emotional state.
It's time to move on and get myself over to the bus stop as this rain is really belting down. Although I am soaking wet, I hope it's like this on all of my adventures. Staying undercover will be a piece of moist cake! Lovely.

Eventually the rain calms down. It's still wet enough for a few people to keep their umbrellas up, but dry enough for me to get going. It's about a 20-minute walk to my next stop and there's a brief stop off on the way so I can get changed. As I've said before, it's all planned out.
Strolling down Artists Way is nice enough. There are a few people dotted about, so I don't look too obvious walking out in the rain. There are even a few kids out playing football and the odd dog walker here and there.
It's just a normal day.

Stepping off Artists Way, I take a right and head toward a wooded area which is an ideal opportunity to get undercover and get myself changed.
Off comes the coat and the hoodie and in its place, a different coloured hoodie and a hat.
As I mentioned before, I'm well prepared.
Next step is to hide my discarded clothes. I was going to dump and set fire to them somewhere in Anton Lakes, but there are so many dog walkers around I can't risk

getting caught so I pop my wet clothes into my rucksack and head off.
I make it to the retail park, which sits as nothing more than an assortment of sterile grey boxes, only recognisable by the corporate branding on the fronts and the sides of the buildings. It's not too busy as the rain seems to have kept most casual shoppers away. This benefits me because when the weather is bad people are going to be finding shelter and that's normally in food places and I can't see many other food places around here, so the chicken place is my best shot. As I enter, it is as busy as I was hoping it would be, so I grab myself a corner of the restaurant and enjoy some chicken and chips. To pass the time, I log into my social media account and see what the world is up to. I do have Instagram but can't be arsed with it most of the time, especially now they've done away with all the self-harm images that used to populate my feed. Instead, I'm left with digital prostitutes and tedious, empty, generic memes to show that someone really cares about you and your mental health. On the back of this there are vast numbers of mongrels that play the **WOE IS ME** card to the maximum. I've seen it. I've seen these accounts grow and they are as tragic as they are pathetic. Posting a selfie of yourself crying or blaming a mental illness because you're too fat and lazy to get up off your arse and do some work. Sadfishing. It's called sadfishing. Being sadder than everyone else so everyone else can boost your ego with comments like **'SENDING LOVE AND HUGS'** or **'YOU CAN GET THROUGH THIS.**

DM ME ANYTIME'.

Fucking spoons.

The fatter you are, the richer you are, the sadder you are, and the thicker you are the better.
Instagram loves that shit. I prefer to use twitter, or X, because it's my pub. X is the landlord and inside are all the distinct groups of people. The people I join at the bar are funny fuckers and open-minded, but the pub is full of all sorts. The far right, the far left, pro-Trump, anti-Trump, armchair activists, comedians, #blacklivesmatter, #whitelivesmatter, #alllivesmatter, all the transtrenders, gender fluid, gender non-conforming, racists, bigots, Fascists, Nazis, Marxists, non-offending paedophiles, zoophiles, necrophiles, basically if you want to find it- X has it. On the big screen there is a wide selection of videos available. Violent videos, football videos, music videos, hate videos, funny videos, porn videos, scat videos, Lolita fantasy videos, furry sex videos and videos from events that are happening in real time that the mainstream media will never show you.
And just like any old pub, it's super easy to get into an argument. Be careful who you pick your fights with, because you could easily find yourself kicked out and barred. Those whose arguments fizzle out quickly will run to the landlord and get you removed. Weakness. I hate weakness.

The other social media accounts I'm not too bothered about. I mean, if Twitter is the pub then Facebook is your mum's house, LinkedIn is the overpriced wine bar down the road full of assholes standing around tossing each other off. Snapchat is the dodgy titty bar and TikTok is the youth centre where creepy bastards hide out in the bushes and jerk off to the young girls dancing around in the tightest of clothes.

As I munch down the last of my chips, a group walk in who are perfect. What I mean by that is that they are the type of people that you would not piss on if they were on fire. Proper scummy little bastards with no respect for anyone, and by the looks of the girls with them, they have no self-respect either. One of these walking bags of shit is going to be my first kill. I am about to pop my murder cherry!

Oh. My. God.

I can't believe I did it, I just did it. My heart is going so fast I don't even know if I'm alive. I think I'm alive. I don't remember getting here. I remember I was in KFC. I followed that one guy to the toilet and now I'm here. Where am I? Where the actual fuck am I?

Salisbury!

Okay, I need to get myself a drink, sit down, calm down and work out what's going on. Coffee! I need coffee. Coffee with coffee, overpriced yes, but it doesn't matter right now. Let's just think this thing through.
I can't. I can't think straight.
Work backwards and get some clarity on this.

OK, I changed in the woods, I walked to the grubby restaurant, I got food and watched these bastards walk in. Fuck, I am shaking.

6. 6. 6.

One of the lads then went to the toilet. He got the code, and I followed right behind. I think I put on an Irish accent when I thanked the attendant for some stupid reason. I don't know why, and as he went into the cubicle I just waited outside. I could hear him snorting so knew what he was up to. As he opened the door, I hit him as hard as I could with the hammer.
He fell back and I hit him again. He wasn't moving, but just to make sure I did it one more time. There was blood everywhere. I don't know what was covered and what wasn't covered, I don't know if I was covered? I don't know, shit! Am I covered?
No, everything looks clean. My shoes are a bit grubby but that's just going to be footprints and I'm wearing the wrong size shoes anyway so that's okay, I'm not bothered about that. Hopefully, I just had my head down.

I can't start second guessing myself. I planned this to the last detail, so I need to have faith in myself.
Holy shit, I just smacked a little fucker in the head with a hammer.
Ok, I need to compose myself and get home, but why am I in Salisbury? To get from Andover and back home there is a train change in Salisbury so that is what happened. Next train is due in fifteen minutes. I need to calm down now and take this moment to breathe.

6. 6. 6.

The train journey from Salisbury to Southampton was strange, I couldn't hear anything. I couldn't hear the train. I couldn't hear the music I was listening to, and I couldn't hear any voices. I couldn't hear anything! I was just in a trance. I had a sense of absolute calm yet amazed at myself. I don't feel guilty. I don't have any regrets.

Yesterday this guy, who we will now call Hammerhead, was making plans for today, making plans for tomorrow, making plans for next week. This morning he woke up, said goodbye to everyone as he normally would, walked down the road, and did whatever he did for the last time. And I made sure that was his last time. I don't know his name and to be honest it doesn't matter; all I know is I'm winning. First point to me!

Tomorrow I will go online and check the Andover Advertiser and see if this has been picked up. My journey has begun.

TWO : BASINGSTOKE

If I had bigger hands, I would be able to carry more Lego and therefore tidy up a lot quicker but, on the downside, I would struggle with the finer details of construction, especially with the tiny single stud pieces. Same problem, but in reverse if I had tiny little hands. Construction would be easy but cleaning up would take longer. Maybe having average sized hands is best?
Fat people use less water when they have a bath but must do more loads in the washing machine because their clothes are so much bigger and take up more space. A skinny person would be able to put more into the washing machine, but then would need to run the bath for longer to get the same coverage as the fat person. So again, is it just best to be average?
Average hands, average weight, average life.
No thanks, not for me. I did that for so long and realised that I am nothing more than a number.
A statistic.
A funeral waiting to happen.
Clothes in a bin bag waiting outside a charity shop.
Photos of moments lost forever in a cardboard box.
Drunk laughs at the bar as people raise another glass in memory of me.
What's the point?

Yes, I've thought about ending my life and have come close on more than one occasion. Many times, I have stood at the top of a flight of stairs and considered overstepping the first step and letting gravity do the rest. Every time I stand on a platform waiting for a train, I think about jumping onto the track right before the train arrives. It would need to be in one of those trains that has the announcement *'the following train is not due to stop at this platform.'* Those bastards come through at some speed so my death would not only be quick but also super messy, and no doubt a talking point for many over the following days. Easy, but I don't want that. I have suicidal tendencies, but I am in control of my life and I'm also in charge of yours. I may have nothing to live for, but I also have nothing to die for, so I am the middleman between life and death.

Arriving at Basingstoke station, I head towards my destination. Once again on foot but this time I'm booked into a nearby hotel. The reason being is this way I can avoid a situation similar to the one in Andover when I freaked out. Can't do that again.
I arrive at reception and make a point that I am here on business. Dressed in a sharp navy-blue suit, pink shirt and super shiny shoes, this is my professional man appearance with, may I add, nicely styled hair and short beard. As far as my personality, I want to be assertive yet polite, wealthy but not arrogant. I want the staff to remember me for all the right reasons when they get asked about guests who stayed here at the same time someone was murdered nearby. I'm trying to hide in plain sight. Like a soldier in a bush, whatever that

means?
I'm booked in for three nights and have a strict timetable to keep to, but not this evening. This evening is about chilling out in my room and watching some TV as tomorrow I'm hosting a business meeting.

It's 4pm and I have just finished the meeting. We held it in the bar, so the event was visible to all staff and I ensured my guests were well looked after. My guests? This morning I booked two male escorts to come to the hotel at 2:45pm, the reason being I was trying to make my ex-boyfriend jealous. I asked that they dress super smart and I would pay them both £400 each for the hour. All they had to do was enjoy my company, and whatever drinks they ordered would get added to my tab.

The first to arrive was Luke, who made a decent effort with a nice grey suit, the type of suit that you could wear to work, a wedding or a funeral. It wasn't flashy, and it wasn't crap, it was just right.
My second guest, Richard, went a bit more business casual with jeans, a black shirt and blazer. Don't get me wrong, they both looked adorable and if my ex-boyfriend actually existed, I'm sure he would have been envious to see me with these two delightfully edible specimens. As we all sat down, I had to clarify that my ex had yet to start his shift, but he would be here soon. I then paid them each their £400, ordered drinks and began chatting. By 3:30pm it was clear that my ex would

not show up but that was ok because Luke and Richard (or Big Dick as he is also known) seem to have forgotten why they are here and are just enjoying a casual chat and free drinks. At 4:20pm I told the guys I had to leave as I had a conference call in ten minutes, but they were welcomed to stay if they wanted and get themselves another drink, on my tab of course. Which they did.

It's now 8pm, and time to mask up.

I have gone with one of the hyper-realistic masks I ordered and honestly, this one is pretty incredible. Paired up with some grey trousers, cheap white trainers (one size too small) and a blue lightweight jacket, I look like an average guy. Clean shaven, slightly chubby and a balding head. I couldn't look more boring. Add some thick-rimmed glasses and I'm sorted. Time to get my new 50+ year old persona out and commit a crime.

Do you know of the band Skid Row? They released a song called Monkey Business and one lyric read 'the freaks come out at nine, it's twenty to ten'
This is so accurate right now as there are plenty of freaks out here this evening. Sounds rich coming from me as I'm the only fool walking around with shoes that are a size too small and a mask on, but no one has looked at me twice so it must be working.

I head towards the car park at Festival Place as this looks like the best place for me to cross B off my list.

Thankfully, I didn't have to wait too long as I spot a guy heading toward the back of the car park. He's on his phone and whoever it is he's talking to is clearly giving him a hard time.
It's ok, I'll sort that out for you telephone person.
As I walk toward him, he finishes his call and looks at me.

You alright mate?

Yes of course, I'm just somewhat confused. I can't remember where I parked.

Ah, I can't help you there.

Maybe you can, I have one of these apps on my phone which helps me locate my car, but I don't know how to use the thing.

Ok, let me have a quick look.

As I move towards him, I can feel my heartbeat increasing and I am getting seriously sweaty under this mask. Is this, nerves? Anxiety? I have to stop and catch my breath and it's at that point the guy walks over to me.

You sure you're alright mate?

He is such a nice guy. Shame I have to kill him.

Once he is in front of me, I lift my head and it's then that he knows something isn't right. Maybe he can spot I'm wearing a mask? Maybe he can see the fear and rage in my eyes? I haven't got time to think about it, so I grip the handle of my knife, pull it out of my pocket and thrust the blade into his throat. Not once, but twice. And again. And again, once more. The guy drops to the floor clutching his neck, but we both know it's pointless. We both know his last remaining minutes on this earth will be spent laying on the floor of a Basingstoke car park watching his neck pissing blood.

What is he staring at? Why do the dying just stare at nothing? It's kind of fascinating but I need to go. Goodnight nice guy.
I turn away and head back to the hotel.

Once back in my room I rip the mask from my head and immediately order room service. Two bottles of beer arrive within a couple of minutes and when I answer the door, I am back in my business attire, minus the shoes and jacket. I have a pre-recorded voice message playing from my phone that makes it appear to the uninitiated that I am on a business call.
I thank the girl delivering my beers and make some comment about having to work past 11pm or something? I remember she said she must do the same, which made me laugh.

I wish her a good night, close my door and crash onto my bed.

Outside, the scream of the sirens signal that the nice guy has been discovered. I hope whoever he was on the phone with can forgive him.

Word of the attack in the car park spreads quickly around the hotel as what looks like the manager stands by the hotel entrance and talks at length with the Police. I make my way to reception to let the young guy behind the desk aware that I have visitors at 2:00pm and if I'm not here at reception, could he please contact me as I'll be in my room.
Of course, there are no visitors at 2pm and I'll make sure I amend that information a little nearer the time, but for now it looks like I am just a regular guest with nothing to hide. I am about to leave the hotel and go for a walk when I am stopped by an officer who is lurking outside. I explain that I'm here on business and will be staying at the hotel again tonight. My whereabouts last night? In my hotel room, on a conference call. The girl on duty last night will confirm, as I spoke to her when I ordered room service. The officer seemed happy with that and informed me that would be in touch should they require any more information.
Down the road I can see the blue and white police tape with officers surrounding the area as passers-by whisper and jump to conclusions about what exactly happened here. A random incident or was the nice guy tied up

with someone or something that could have triggered this brutal attack? I hope so, that would really help. I need to stop, I'm hungry.

I'm on my way home now.
Three nights in Basingstoke was more than enough considering the circumstances. It was fascinating watching the different types of people dealing with this unexpected news. From the Police to the hotel staff and public, everyone has a different trigger level, a different way of coping with stress, a different perspective of life and death.

Me? I couldn't give a shit. He's dead and I'm on my way out of Basingstoke, right under the noses of the same people who are trying to find me.
The train journey back is peaceful and has given me a rare chance to reflect. Not on my recent actions in Basingstoke, but on how I even got here in the first place, but it isn't long before I am distracted.
Reflect.
Reflection.

I'm a reflection of your negative.

Do you know who said that?
In 1981, 60 Minutes Australia interviewed Charles Manson from California State Prison in Corcoran. It was being reported that this was his first interview since he had been locked up following the multiple murders

committed by his family in 1969. In the late 1960s Manson created the Manson Family and at its peak is believed to have had around 50 followers with most of the group being young, white women from middle-class backgrounds. Anyway, none of that is important and I'm sure you know who Charles Manson is. I mean, you know who Jesus is, right? Well, they are one of the same.

During the interview, the topic of Manson's release was discussed, but the public opinion was that they would hope Manson would never see freedom as they were afraid that he would kill again. Manson's response;

Again? I think you guys are misinformed. I haven't killed anyone.

Are these the words of someone in denial? Shifting blame elsewhere because he does not believe that he indulged in those crimes. Is he perhaps just playing us and creating good TV? Making a statement like this will keep people talking about him even though he has been long removed from the public eye. Was he crazy? Insane? Mentally ill? Or was he a genius?

On November 19, 2017, Charles Manson died and cremated. But I don't think he was. I think some of the most notorious names to walk across our green Earth such as Manson, Dahmer, Gacy, Shipman, Bundy, Bin Laden, Hussain, and even Hitler have their remains stored away somewhere. Those who faced death by lethal injection didn't die at all. John-Wayne Gacy and the Angel of Death herself, Aileen Wuornos, were just knocked unconscious. Propofol is used to do the deed and then once the show was over, the bodies got transported to some secret underground science place, resuscitated, experimented on, and their DNA used to create a toxin that when injected into pregnant women, made their babies super evil. These babies and their families received unwanted attention from mysterious people that hid within the shadows, and without them knowing, they controlled their lives with each baby being assigned a task before birth. People like Dzokhar Tsarnaev (Boston Marathon Bomber) were injected with the evil toxin whilst in the womb and then carefully manipulated until that day in Boston in 1993 when he helped in the murder of three people and injuring over two hundred others.

I should give lectures on this in universities. Not the good universities, but the shittier ones where all you need to gain a place is the ability to wake up in the morning and spell your name correctly. Actually no, not universities. There are way too many wankers in that environment, and I do not mix well with others. Maybe be an online tutor? No, I don't think that would work for me either. I like to look into the eyes of those I speak to. I don't buy into the bullshit that the eyes are the windows to the soul because we have no soul, but there is certainly something hidden within the eyes. I do not know what because we are nothing more than germs, cells, chemicals. Skeletons with skin and muscle and one very vital component, the brain. Our bodies are the vessels and within that our brain controls everything. How well that works depends on our experiences and what we are exposed to from those early days.

I wish this train would hurry up and get me home. I'm getting agitated now. We're just pulling into Winchester so not long to go.

THREE : CAMBRIDGE

Mental health is funny isn't it. All you have to do is talk about it and the stigma, is reduced!
That's right, just by having a conversation online we can help reduce the stigma around mental health. It's as easy as that!
Written words that are so powerful, that no matter how far gone you may feel you are the right sentence, inspirational quote or virtual hug will pull you right out of that dark place and back into the light. What a wonderful world we live in! From the comfort of our armchairs, we can change the world and save lives. Well done you and well done us.
I hope my sarcastic tone is getting through to you on this one.

Reel it back in for a minute and indulge in the idea that mental health isn't the problem. We all have mental health. Mental health + physical health = health.
The stigma that exists is around mental ill health. Mental illness. Mental disorders.
I watched a program the other day where one millionaire spoke to another millionaire about depression. Millionaire #1 was really honest about his struggles and enforced the fact that opening up and seeking help helped him get through that dark part of his life. Millionaire #2 expressed real empathy in front of the cameras and together they showed us that now is

the right time to be open and honest about our mental health, and that is amazing. Let us all get together and talk about our mental health, to seek help and support. In the meantime, this interview gives every one of us the chance to jump online, use the relevant hashtag and quote stuff like;

You are so strong, you can get through this.
Don't give up. You can win this battle.
You are so much more than your diagnosis.
Talk about your mental health, it's so important.

It's so tedious watching people indulge in verbal intercourse with one another. The same phrases, the same memes the same selection of heart and hug emojis. How does sending a virtual hug gif, help anyone! We think we are helping and maybe we are helping the lonely and needy members of our digital society, but the people that really need help are ignored. We are scared to talk to these people because they are on the edge and try as we might, we do not understand that they are on the brink of unimaginable horror and self-inflicted mutilation. It could be their physical being or what hides beneath. The mental anguish, torture and violent outbursts that look like nothing more than a mood swing, but inside this person is hurting. Screaming. Crying. Dying.

Going back to the millionaire who inspired us all on TV. Yes, he had mental illness but, and this is a big BUT, he also had access to immediate support and treatment.

Remember, mental illness does not discriminate, but access to treatment does.

Three months I waited for an appointment with a mental health professional after I had reached out and opened up. Three months. Do you have any idea how hard it is not to die whilst waiting that long? Do you have any idea how much it hurts to be told that you are a priority case, but it's still going to take up to TWELVE WEEKS to be seen. I know across the UK the waiting times can be even longer, but not if you're rich!
Get your wealthy ass on TV, tell everyone all about your sad fucking story and watch those virtuous armchair dwellers get to work.

Question for you.
Have you sat there, week after week, talking to a fucking trainee psychologist as part of a recovery program you were forced to attend because it's the only therapy / help available right now and then a few weeks into these sessions have them put you on a two-week break because they need to investigate your past over comments that you made? No, I didn't think so.
This is exactly what happened to me, which was horrific, especially as I had listed paranoia as one of my issues. I remember explaining in great detail how I was once getting extremely uncomfortable in a supermarket checkout queue because the packs of biscuits behind

me kept talking and whispering when I wasn't looking. I get paranoid when animals look at me. I'm sure cats have built in video capture. I don't like it when people walk past me and are smiling independently. What are they smiling about? Are they laughing at me? What's wrong with my face? Why are they laughing?

After all of this, they still then had the audacity to tell me to not come back for two weeks as they had to look into the statement I had made about my past.

For the record, they found nothing because nothing happened, but for those two weeks I was on the edge. My paranoia was unmanageable, and every day felt like I'd lived five.

Second guessing myself and convinced I'd done something wrong, yet I knew I had done nothing wrong, but these professionals looked at it a different way and destroyed whatever progress had been made toward me getting better.

After the two weeks I went back, and they confirmed that there was no police record or any other charges against me, so it is ok to carry on with the therapy sessions.

I could not be a part of this any longer. I told them I would not be coming back after the way they made me feel. They weren't overly concerned. In fact, I'd say they couldn't really care less. After all, I am just a number. A weekly appointment that exists just to get the boxes ticked. If I walked out of that door today and never came back, there would be plenty of other nut jobs ready to take my place. I mean, there is hardly a

shortage of mentally ill people is there.
Now, I could go on about the constant meetings and assessments with various psychologists, psychiatrists, and others who have tried to teach me mindfulness or meditation.
I could go on about the various combinations of medicines they have prescribed me.
Escitalopram, sertraline, quetiapine to name a few. I am still on high dosage medication now and have been for 18 months, maybe? I'm not too sure. It's been over a year. It might be pushing two years? Possibly 30 months, I honestly have no idea. All I know is I take those little white oblongs every morning, and it's supposed to do something.
Whatever it does it hasn't stopped me from killing two people and today, I am going to make it three.

There is a protest happening in Cambridge and what the protest is about I couldn't give a toss, but I'm not there to parade my virtue upon others. I'm here to tick C off the list and enjoy myself.
My journey to Cambridge means I have to change at Waterloo, which is great as I will easily blend into the hundreds of other people buzzing around. I'm travelling light today. Clothes, hoodie, and a rucksack. In the rucksack are two bottles of water, two bars of chocolate, two OTF knives, a change of clothes, oh and of course, some baby wipes and the letter C from my

alphabet book. Have I mentioned the Alphabet book yet?

As I walk through Waterloo station, I head down to the toilets to relieve myself and head to the same cubicle I always use when I'm in this part of the world. Fourth cubicle on the left-hand side as you walk in, that's mine. They have cleaned it since the last time I was here; I know because I smeared a massive bogey against the silver poster frame last time I visited and it's not there anymore. I'm sure the cleaners have removed worse from these cubicles. For a major UK train station, the toilets are always pretty gross. They stink of stale piss and there are bits of wet tissue paper everywhere. The urinal right next to the hand drier is where I think the gays meet up. There is no other reason a urinal would be that close to where you dry your hands. Unless it's for people who are in a rush so just dry their hands whilst they piss? Either way, cubicle number 4 is mine.

I'm just a few minutes away from Cambridge station now and from there, Kings Parade is about a mile or so away. Easy 25 minute stroll through Cambridge but as I get closer to my destination, I realise that I am about to be a part of a climate change protest. Fuck me, here we go. Another day out for the middle classes to shout and scream about something that will never be taken seriously. Look beyond the borders of your own country dickheads, some cardboard signs and catchy tunes will not stop the major pollution powerhouses.

Sir, we need to stop production on all of our things that make pollution. The reason being is because the organic couscous brigade are waving signs about and chaining themselves to lampposts.

The walk to Kings Parade is nice enough, but as I get closer, so does the noise. I dislike protests like this. It's a bandwagon, and that's all it will ever be. Journalists and photographers everywhere as events like this are perfect for creating exaggerated stories and boosting the advertising revenue through clickbait.

I'm in the thick of the protest now and as I trudge through the crowd, I pass by a kid who is holding up half a cardboard box on which he has scribbled
'save our planet. it's the only one with chocolate'.
I really wanted to explain to this little prick the journey of the average West African cocoa bean, the volume of air miles, the production, carbon emissions or whatever, but I thought better of it. It would no doubt draw needless attention to me, and his mother doesn't look like the type who enjoys a good debate. I smile and move on through the crowd.

The good thing about crowds like this is the noise. So much noise that a scream in agony will not create attention, and even if the few around the victim realise what is going on, there will be so much commotion that no one will know where to start, and this is where I would make my slow yet deliberate escape.

If you can't re-use it. Refuse it.
Are the words scrawled across a piece of A2 sized card and held aloft by one of those exact people I spoke about on my way up here. The sanctimonious, virtue signaling, middle class bags of white privileged shit. She stands there right in front of me waiting to be immortalised as my third victim, so why should I deny her that right. As I walk closer, she shouts along with the crowd.
For her, this is a wonderful day out. A chance to release the frustrations she keeps tucked away as her husband continues his affair with Oscar and Bunty's Swiss au pair. She knows this is happening but lets it pass as she cannot afford to be without his income. She would lose her home, her family, and also her status and would no longer be a part of this community she so dearly loves. It doesn't matter that she no longer knows who she is as she is living a grand life. A life that she has been told many times, is perfect. Shame it ends today.

I'm right behind her now, so close I can taste her scent. I pretend that someone nudges me from behind and I fall into the back of her. I apologise but she doesn't hear me. I stay close and in each hand; I have my OTF knives, with the safety off of course. As I lean ever closer to her, I flick the switches and the blades spring out. I take a deep breath and pretending yet again that the crowd has pushed me, I fall into her and push the knives in as deep as I can. Left side and right side, double penetration. I keep the blade in my right hand deep within her tissue and with the serrated edge I push down as hard as I can. With my left hand, I pull the blade out and stab again. She becomes limp in my arms and a lot sooner than I was expecting. Don't know if she made a noise or not because someone decided now would be a good time to blow an air horn. Shame, as I wanted to hear her moan as I got deeper into her than anyone has ever done before. Tearing through skin and into her internal organs, I wanted to hear her last breath. I wanted to see if the soul flies out of your mouth when you die. Fuck, dead people are really heavy. It's time to get out of here and let her fall.

As I yank the blades away, I feign a fall backwards and scream for help. Within seconds people have noticed what has happened. Panic and fear have gripped the crowd as the dead woman is motionless on the floor just a few feet away from me. Someone in the crowd helps me up and asks if I'm ok.

What? No! What happened. Oh my god, what is happening.

The helpful stranger steps aside as I move gingerly away. An onsite paramedic attempts to breathe life into the dead woman, but they can tell it's already too late. I continue to drift along with the crowd, knives in my gloved hands, blades retracted and firmly in my pockets.

Not a single person knows that the weapons used to kill this woman are just inches from their bodies. I could easily strike again but I need to keep this to what it is; one kill, one letter. C is complete, so it is time to move on.

I notice a young guy who has his rucksack open whilst he is sipping water from a bottle. The bag is on the floor and he is unaware that I am moving closer.

I nudge past him, politely but firmly, and as I do, I drop one of my knives into his open bag. Hopefully that will keep the authorities busy when they find the knife wielding maniac just a few feet away from the scene.

I bet this protest will now get the media attention it craves. If you want people to talk, give them something to talk about. Cardboard slogans and shouting achieve nothing. Remember, actions speak louder than words.

FOUR : VULTURE

I must have been around four years old when I took part in my school's Easter Bonnet Parade. There are only three words to this event–Easter Bonnet Parade. Yet I was the only kid to turn up in a mask. I remember my mum making it on the eve of the parade and I watched in awe as she transformed an empty cornflakes box into a fluffy bunny rabbit mask. But, as amazing as it was, I was still the only kid in a fucking mask.

It took another fifteen years or so before I realised the beauty and power of a mask, and from that moment on, I never stopped collecting. From the crap £1 versions that you get from the pound shops every Halloween to the high end, hyper realistic silicone masks that are shipped in from the US and cost more than £1200 a go but you know what, throw on a wig, sunglasses, and a hat and suddenly you become just like everybody else. Another face in the crowd.

By wearing a mask, I could explore my dark side without regret as I felt I had become a totally different person. More confident, more aggressive, and more, me. Even though I am me, I am not me until I am hidden.
The real me is better and stronger than the real me, yet to be fair I don't really like either of them. What I like even less are people. We think we are something more than what we really are, yet we are nothing but

disposable moments. None of us are born equal and we live with this fact, until death. Death brings equality. Imagine 7 billion electric pulses darting along 7 billion wires. Approximately 55 million of those electric pulses will burn out over the course of a year only to be replaced by 84 million new ones. Every year the same pattern, the same process, until one day the circuit board will no longer be able to function. When that happens, all the lights will fade. We return to black and at that point, we are all equal.

Thomas Edison, was once described as America's greatest inventor, died in 1931. He was born in 1847. Everyone who was born in 1847 is now dead. All of them, dead. You can argue that Edison left behind a legacy, a chance for humanity to progress and develop bigger and greater things, but he is still dead.
David Bowie is dead. He was an incredible artist and his music touched the hearts and ignited the minds of millions, but he is still dead. One day all of his fans will be dead, and then what? He will be nothing more than a trivia question or a statue.

Tina Turner. Marc Bolan. Jimi Hendrix. Karen Carpenter. Muddy Waters. Frank Zappa. Kenny Rogers. Lemmy. Eazy-E. Fats Domino. John Denver. Taylor Hawkins. Glenn Miller. Frank Sinatra. Cecil Womack. Sonny Bono. Michael Hutchence. Janis Joplin. Ella Fitzgerald. Tony Allen. Eddie Van Halen. Miles Davis. Nat 'King' Cole. Prince. Marvin Gaye. Phil Lynott. Tom Petty. Gordon

Haskell. Linda McCartney. 2Pac. Chris Cornell. Barry White. Joey Ramone. Ronald Bell. Roy Orbison. Errol Brown. Johnny Cash. Bon Scott. Leonard Cohen. Freddie Mercury. John Entwistle. Nina Simone. B.B.King. Kurt Cobain. John Lee Hooker. Billie Holiday. Jim Morrison. Bill Haley. Dr.Feelgood. Keith Flint. Ian Dury. Luciano Pavarotti. Andy Williams. Kirsty MacColl. Louis Armstrong. Gene Pitney. Spencer Davis. Isaac Hayes. Amy Winehouse. Keith Moon. George Harrison. Donna Summer. Bob Marley. Maurice Gibb. Coolio. Ray Charles. Little Richard. Joe Strummer. Bill Withers. Malcolm McLaren. Ronnie James Dio. The Big Bopper. Michael Jackson. Robert Palmer. John Bonham. Aretha Franklin. Chester Bennington. Brian Jones. Eddie Cochran. John Lennon. Johnny Ramone. Otis Reading. Patsy Cline. Luther Vandross. Robin Gibb. Lou Reed. Whitney Houston. Gene Wilder. Aaliyah. Buddy Holly. John Belushi. Elvis Presley. Audrey Hepburn. Marlon Brando. Peter O'Toole. Cary Grant. John Candy. Bette Davis. Tony Curtis. Vincent Price. Paul Newman. Jackie Stallone. Thomas Jefferson Byrd. Adam West. Ray Liotta. Katharine Hepburn. Greta Garbo. Charlie Chaplin. Charlton Heston. Bernie Mac. Leslie Nielsen. Michael Clarke Duncan. Heath Ledger. Janet Leigh. Roger Moore. Farrah Fawcett. John Hurt. Bruce Lee. Vivien Leigh. Paul Walker. Henry Fonda. Jean Harlow. Marilyn Monroe. Robin Williams. Christopher Reeve. Patrick Swayze. Angela Lansbury. Sam Lloyd. Dennis Farina. Jack Lemmon. Leonard Nimoy. Natalie Wood. Brittany Murphy. Heather O'Rourke. Robbie Coltrane. Rip Torn.

George Peppard. Peter Fonda. Burt Reynolds. Humphrey Bogart. Ingrid Bergman. John Wayne. Sean Connery. Sharon Tate. Robert Vaughn. Steve McQueen. Michael Gambon. Carl Reiner. Telly Savalas. Walter Matthau. Roy Scheider. Gregory Peck. Fred Astaire. Richard Pryor. Carrie Fisher. Larry Hagman. Chadwick Boseman. Rutger Hauer. Dana Plato. Marty Feldman. Chris Farley. Peter Mayhew. Dennis Hopper. Honor Blackman. Elizabeth Taylor. Oliver Reed. Dame Diana Rigg. Doris Day. Clark Gable. Mae West. Lucille Ball. Yul Brynner.Mickey Rooney. Bill Paxton. Verne Troyer. Judy Garland. Alan Rickman. Rita Hayworth. James Dean. Geoffrey Palmer. Luke Perry. Richard Harris. Corey Haim. Kenneth Williams. Christopher Lee. Lisa Marie Presley. Grace Kelly. Sid James. John Sessions. Dudley Moore. Davy Jones. Peter Sellers. Bobby Ball. Rik Mayall. Eddie Large. Peter Cook. Spike Milligan. Ronnie Barker. Eric Morcambe. Clive Swift. Frank Windsor. Tommy Cooper. Dave Allen. Ronnie Corbett. Benny Hill. Les Dawson. Tim Brooke-Taylor. Victoria Wood. Graham Chapman. Cleopatra. Winston Churchill. Adolf Hitler. Margaret Thatcher. Queen Victoria. JFK. Ruth Bader Ginsburg. Robert Mugabe. Abraham Lincoln. Ronald Reagan. Martin Luther King. Jacques Chirac. Li Peng. Mahatma Ghandi. Genghis Khan. Dame Vera Lynn. Nelson Mandela. Mother Teresa. David Bellamy. Harold Wilson. Oliver Cromwell. Pol Pot. Osama Bin Laden. Sadako Ogata. Otto Von Bismarck. Kim Bok-dong. Boris Yeltsin. John Wayne Gacy. Mary Ann Cotton. John Lynch. William Burke. Fred West. William Hare. Jeffrey

Dahmer. John Christie. Ian Brady. Charles Manson. Vladimir Romanov. Harold Shipman. Jack the Ripper.

The list can go on and on, but I think you understand my point. They are all dead. They leave behind a mark on this world, be it positive or negative, yet they are still dead.
Their moment has passed and although the names will live on in the bowels of the internet, the impact they have on all of our tomorrows will become less and less important as we create new heroes and new villains.

We mourn strangers from the comfort of our smart phones. We hashtag the latest cause hoping it will change the world. It won't. In a world where everyone is connected, we have never been so far apart.
When we stand and pause for breath, we stand divided. Divided by religion, hatred, race and money. The rich at the top and everyone else below. Yes, I have money, but I'm not rich. I am equal to you. I don't care if you're the company CEO or the toilet cleaner; you are a person and I will treat you as such, but if you think it's ok to disrespect me, then you can quite simply fuck off.

Three days ago, I walked the same streets I walked as a kid when out delivering newspapers. It was nice catching up with my old self and I felt inspired to write so I headed to the Prince of Wales pub, grabbed a pint and put pen to paper.

Walking my paper round
Twenty years later
Listening to the same music
Walking the same streets

Everything has changed
The letterboxes are lower
The stairwells much tighter
I'm glad *that* dog is dead

The homes are smaller
The roads much shorter
The shops are just shells
But the pavement still smells

Old brick and new brick
Sit side by side
A brand-new eyesore
Never complimentary

The nursery's a centre for the kids of the kids
Who again have had kids, who again are now pregnant

Indians have gone
Now Eastern Europeans
Where once stood bikes
Now wheelie bins

How did I play on these roads with my friends?

So narrow the space, so grey and uninspiring

Yet this was home
I walk so I remember
Not everything was perfect
But it was never supposed to be

Once I'd finished my pint, I had another pint, chatted to a couple of the locals and then had another pint. It's polite to stay when someone buys you a drink plus, I think he wanted to bone me but that will not happen, not after just three pints anyway. As much as my new friend Clifford wanted me to stay, I felt it was time to go. I had a pretty good day up to this point, so didn't want to ruin it with some unnecessary bum business. With a couple of pints in my belly and a phone number I'll never ring, I felt good so decided to head towards one of the many council estates that are contained within the city boundaries.
Last time I was here, some woman said she would suck my dick for £20. Nothing happened because I didn't have any money. If I had £20, I would have let her and I'm sure I would have enjoyed it. Could have made it a regular thing, but it didn't happen, so no point dwelling on it.
As I walked between the high-rise tower blocks, I paused and took £100 out of my wallet. I approached a young mixed-race woman and her two kids, who looked like they were both below the age of three.

Excuse me.

What? Who are you?

Sorry, no need to panic I just need to give you something. You dropped it when you walked past me.

I didn't walk past you.

You did. I saw you and this fell out of your bag or the buggy.

What is it.

Money. About £100 I think.

What are you on?

Seriously this is yours.

Are you some kind of fucking pervert?

No, look. If you don't want it then I'll give it to someone else.

It ain't mine.

Yes I know that I was just hoping you'd be less aggressive.

What do you want?

Nothing. I just want you to have this, please.

Is this real money.

Yes. Look, I used to live here, and I know what it's like growing up in places like this. It can be hard. Take it.

And you don't want nothing.

No. I will walk away now. Just look after your babies.

Oh they ain't mine fam.

What.

Yeah they ain't mine. They belong to my sister. I'm just looking after them whilst she, you know, earns a living.

Will you pass the money onto her.

Does she know you.

Just take care of yourself and your family.

Does she know you. Creeping round here giving money to me and not telling me who you are. Fucking creep.

Hang on, I'm going to walk away now ok and let's just leave it there.

As I turn and walk away, I regret giving her that money. I must have travelled no more than 10 paces when I hear her voice once again. This time louder and more aggressive which means there is a man, or men, near her and she is doing that thing bitches do when they just scream. Must be something we did back in our primitive days. If there was a problem in the cave then the woman would start screaming and making a shitload of inaudible noise to get the attention of the man who would then club the problem over the head.

Without looking back I know what is happening, she has male support now and he/they are going to be after me so I did what any serial killer in training would do. I hid in the bins. What I mean is, at the bottom of the high-rise blocks are the refuse areas. Usually hidden away behind a metal shutter, but today the shutters are open.

As I squat next to a couple of shitty nappies and a decapitated barbie doll, I wait and watch. The two men who were looking for me have just walked past. One is a skinny white guy in a bad tracksuit. The other cuts a more intimidating figure. By that I mean he's a slightly fatter black guy in a pair of jeans and football shirt.

Arsenal shirt I think, not that it matters.
I wait for about 30 seconds then make my way out of the bins. I can see the two guys standing and talking to a woman outside a tower block further down the road. No sign of the one who has my £100. Hopefully she has gone to buy baby milk and nappies. I doubt it, but let's hope so.

As I watch them talking, I open my bag and take out another £100. I always carry large wads of cash with me because you never know what could happen and I'm pretty sure I can resolve any conflict with money.
I put the £100 on the floor and slide an OTF knife up each sleeve. I stand and wait for them to turn around, which doesn't take too long.

You looking for me?

Yes mate. What the fuck you doing giving my sister money.

I thought I was doing a nice deed. Clearly I was wrong.

Yes mate you got it totally wrong and because you're a dirty little creep I'm going to fucking hurt you.

Ok, hear me out. You have two options.

You threatening me!

I repeat, you have two options.

What two options.

Look down there. There is £100 on the floor. Take it and fuck off or leave it and I will kill both of you. Right here, right now.

Who the fuck are you?

It doesn't matter, but I suggest you take the money and walk away.

I release the blades from my knives and wait for their next move. This is getting tense.

You think you a big man cos you got a couple of blades.

How about I take your money then I kill you.

Try it. The money is there, and I am here.

The smaller guy walks over and picks up the money as the bigger guy walks over to me. As he approaches, I tell him that one of the kids is mine.
This creates a moment of confusion in his mind, which is enough of a distraction for me to slice across his face with the blade in my left hand and hold the blade in my right, close to his neck.

Take the money and fuck off.

Who are you?

Take the money and fuck off.

Ok man. Back up yeah.

The skinny white guy has already legged it, and Arsenal boy is not amused. He backs off from me and crouches on the floor pressing his hand hard against his newly torn cheek.

Look, I'm just protecting my family yeah.

I don't care what you think you're doing. Walk away so I can go home and pretend this shit never happened.

My face.

Fuck your face.

You really the baby's daddy?

No.

You're fucking weird.

Fuck off and enjoy the money. You and your sister just made £200 for doing nothing. Spend it wisely because I may come back.

If you come back, I'll be ready and we can do this again but next time…

I'll stop you there, you need to pray I don't come back. If I do, I will fly in with such venom that you will not stand a chance.

I'm connected. We all connected here.

Really. Well, where are they now?

With that the prick received a swift kick in the face as I pick up my bag and walked on. I could hear him continue his abuse and threats as I got further and further away from this shit hole. I honestly went there with good intentions, yet it was just thrown back in my face. Ungrateful bastards. I mean what I said, and I have now earmarked this place as my letter S and if I return, they better still be here.

When we stand and pause for breath, we stand divided. Divided by religion, hatred, race and money. The rich at the top and everyone else below. I tried to bridge that gap and it was met with threats of violence and abuse. I try to walk a line that is non-judgmental and totally respectful of other people's opinions and beliefs, but then moments like that happen and it makes me think, why the fuck do I bother. I try to be nice and do things for my fellow man, but it gets thrown back in my face, time and time again. I'm sick of it. Being surrounded by weak, pathetic people who only want to know you because they want something. Well, want do you want from me now! If I gave you everything it wouldn't be enough, so that's why I stand alone. The only person I have to answer to is me, so fuck you and your society. This is why I have become what I have become. I am the black vulture. I am not just right wing and left wing; I am the whole. The body, the heart, the mind. The whole fucking creature. Resourceful, perceptive and cunning. Hunting when I need to and feeding off of the scraps that society leaves behind whenever the opportunity presents itself. Picking away at the foundation of whatever you think you've built, only for it to crumble. An ugly creature by design yet built for purpose. I am not that scabby, club footed pigeon I used to think I was. I am more than that. I am the vulture. My moment on this planet may be brief but I have a moment and I will use my moment to change your moment, forever.

FIVE : DONCASTER

The Letter D

Dejection
Desolation
Desperation
Days are painted for me
Don't ask how I feel
Damaged
Dangerous
Destructive
Dark thoughts bring me comfort
Detailed and vivid
Disgusting
Diseased
Disturbing
Devotion to failure
Disposable truths
Dying
Denying
Deception
Defeated by pain
Depression has won

I write little poems and such when my brain needs to be kept occupied. It is something I've always done, not because I want to become a great poet alongside the likes of Keats, Milton and Wordsworth, but because I need to work certain emotions out of my system. Nothing I write is contrived to achieve a certain level of critical acclaim. I do it just to please myself and keep my brain active for a few minutes.

I found myself at the hospital
Surrounded by amputees
I looked at those who have no hands
I wonder how they feel

When I was a kid, I used to wander round a hospital near to where I lived and slap the empty beds left abandoned in the corridors. I was on my own and I think I must have been between 9-10 years old? Thinking back, do you remember those things your nan probably used to hang from her front room door or kitchen door to stop the flies getting in? They were strips of colourful plastic or wooden bead effect hanging things. Always got tangled up round your neck when you tried to walk through them. It looked shit and was super dangerous, but they were a home necessity once upon a time. Well, the same applied to this hospital I used to walk about in, but instead of colourful plastic strips or beads they would have these thick, grey, heavy, PVC door flaps measuring about 30cm in width, hanging in between rooms and corridors. Hideous things, but I used to enjoy playing with them. Lifting them up and letting them drop, time and time again. I was such a lonely child, but I don't think I was unhappy, well not at that point in time. I liked my own company, and the same is true now. I'm more than happy to sit on my own at home or in a pub. I don't need other people around me. With people come problems and sharing. Opinions become diluted as we accept the opinions of others, and in an attempt to feel accepted, we change our views. We no longer have the ability to think independently and become nothing more than a reflection of our peers. I like to think independently, have my own perspective, and play my own games.

I did that once when I was travelling to Belfast. I thought I'd play a game of looking shifty at the airport, which is a one player game and turns out is utter rubbish. The game exists entirely in your own head and it involves seeking out the CCTV, trying to spot the plain clothes security and forgetting to remove certain items when you have to throw all your belongings into the plastic boxes before they go through the Xray machine thing. This was great fun until I got selected at random to be searched by security. As I went through the rectangle doorway it started beeping. So, I went back and took off the dog tags round my neck. Went through and it beeped again. After confirming that I had no metal pins or anything in my body, they let me through, where I was met by a miserable looking Irishman who told me I had been randomly selected and would need to cooperate.
They found nothing except a load of attitude from me, and that was that. I made my way to the departure lounge and waited for the plane back to England.

Manchester airport was a different story. This time I behaved myself, but I still got pulled over for a random search. Really! Random, is it? I tried my best to be polite, but the piss pot searching me was having none of it.
I had to complete a form about why I was visiting Manchester, what was in my bags, and then to top it all off he confiscated my Police Eau de Cologne spray. I loved that spray. Not only did it smell good, but best of all the bottle was shaped like a skull. The Manc piss pot took the spray off for testing, then came back and informed me they have confiscated the man perfume because it contained an ingredient that is not permitted on planes. I sniffed the air. It wasn't Police Eau de Cologne spray I could smell it was bullshit! I could smell bullshit. I asked him what the illegal ingredient was, and he informed me he could not share that information. Yeah, because that information doesn't fucking exist. You just wandered off, sprayed it, had a little sniff and thought, yeah I'll have that, thieving prick.
Since then I have made a point of avoiding airports. Not only do they have all my information documented including my eyeballs and all the other stuff they photograph and scan, they also check your luggage. Sounds basic, but this doesn't happen on a train. I can travel with a suitcase full of weapons on any train I like, yet I've had my Eau de Cologne confiscated by airport security. I'll travel by train then, thank you very much. Slip in and slip out of any city or town in the UK totally unchecked and bring with me whatever I like. The only

downside though being the time it takes to get there, but that's ok because it gives me time to get my mind in the right space and to just, enjoy the moment.

The train journey to Doncaster was long. Enjoy the moment he said, fuck me this took hours! A couple of changes along the way yes, but it is still over 5 hours of travelling. On the way up here I did give some thought and consideration to the idea of being a northerner and speaking the lingo, 'Ow Do, ta'ra, nowt, scran and all that but I thought better of it and decided to stick my original plan of being a visiting American Great Grandson to a lady called Margaret (Maggie or Mags) Bench, who moved to Doncaster with her late husband Dillard toward the back end of the 1970s. She stayed in Doncaster when he died but the family have lost contact with her over the past few months and have become concerned, so I flew over from Washington to track her down. Her last known residence was St. James Street, DN1 3AZ.
The reason for such an elaborate story will become clear but one thing I want to be sure is that my attacks at first appear utterly random and although I leave a clue at the scene, I don't want the authorities to work out too soon that the 26 random deaths across the UK are all linked.

On leaving the station, I head straight towards St Sepulchre Gate and within a couple of minutes I can see my destination. As with every station, I have planned my route well in advance, so I don't look like a tourist when I first walk out onto the streets on whichever city or town I visit. It doesn't matter that I've never been here before because Google maps exists. Some of the imagery or street views are maybe a year or two outdated, but the locations haven't moved. The streets may look a little different, but the names are the same and so far, it hasn't let me down. Thanks, Big G.

When I arrive on St. James street it feels so familiar, yet I've never been here before. It just has the same overcrowded yet empty feel that all estates like this have. I grew up on one and moved into others as I got older and this place is no different. Same shaped buildings, same colours, and I'm sure the same mix of people. The same single mums, old people and low earners. Drug addicts, alcoholics and young families. That's one thing you're guaranteed in a place like this, diversity.

I don't mean the office politics type of diversity where every business has to have within their ranks at least one lesbian, one trans, a black and a disabled. I mean proper, real-life diversity.

I make my way down St. James Street and head towards one of three, 14 storey tower blocks in the area, which are altogether home to, I would say, at least 400 people. Plenty of witnesses, but also plenty of opportunities to blend into the crowds, should I need to.

My first job is to make a phone call to a local escort. The

first two ladies declined to meet at the agreed time and place, but the young woman I contacted after was more than willing. Especially as I mentioned to her that I would be paying double. The time is now 2:45pm and I have booked her for 4pm to meet me and I'll let her know nearer the time from where, but it will be in the vicinity of St. James Street.
This gives me an hour to get this done.

I hover at a safe distance by the tower blocks, pretending to be having a conversation on my phone, and it's not long until an elderly woman clutching a penguin patterned umbrella makes her way towards me. As she gets nearer, we make eye contact. I smile, introduce myself, and begin my story. She had never heard of or met Maggie Bench, but she let me into her building so I can continue my search. I thank her (Winny) at the lift door and I head towards the stairs. As the lift door closes, I walk back to the lobby so I can see which floor she is getting off at. Floor six. I take the stairs and head up to the 12th floor.

The time is now 3:37pm, and I have sat here on the concrete steps for about fifteen minutes. I text the escort and ask her to make her way to the 6th floor of Cusworth House to meet me at 4pm. She instantly replies with a yes. Now is the time to put my thick-rimmed glasses and black baker boy hat back on and head down to catch up with Winny. I'll be glad to get home tomorrow as I will finally get the shave off my

beard and cut my hair. I've been growing them both now for about a year and it just doesn't suit me.
I'm on floor 6 and I can see leaning against one of the doors is the penguin patterned umbrella. I approach the door and give it a little knock.

Hello, who is it?

Um yeah, hello I was wondering if you could help me. I'm trying to find someone called Margaret Bench who used to live in this building. I'm her...

The door opens.

Hello again Eric.

Oh, hey Winny. Sorry I didn't realise this was your apartment.

I guess you haven't had much luck then?

Nope. Everyone that I've spoken to has been really nice but have never heard of her. I think I have the wrong place. Maybe I'm in totally the wrong town? Someone suggested I should perhaps be in Dorchester?

Come in Eric, come in and I'll fix you up with a nice strong brew.

Thanks Winny, that's very kind of you.

Foolish, but kind.

Entering her flat I look at my watch, it's 3.55pm. This box she calls her home is nothing short of a memorial to the past. Photos of smiling people and happy moments. A fat black and white cat is asleep on the sofa and a smaller version of the fat one sits on the chair opposite. Although she has a couple of cats, her place doesn't have that ammoniacal odour of stale piss floating in the air

Um, Winny do you mind if I stand out on your balcony as I'm feeling rather flustered and could do with some fresh air.

Course you can, but I'm not sure how fresh the air will be as we're right next to the road.

That's ok, I just need to collect my thoughts.

Ok duck. I'll bring your drink out to you.

She called me DUCK. Donald Duck? Toilet Duck? Rubber Duck? I tell you what, when she gets out here, she had better not duck!

It's 4pm, where's the fucking tea.

A couple minutes later she finally joins me on the balcony. I thank her and take my cup. The liquid inside

looks disgusting. I think they call it builders tea or something. It's basically a strong cup of tea with a noticeable lack of milk. I dip my finger into it and yeah, it's hot.
I turn to face Winny and before she has a chance to open her mouth, I throw the contents of my cup right into her face. The hot scalding liquid making contact with her skin, her lips, her open eyes. She doesn't scream but makes a strange noise that I would imagine an asthmatic would make if they were trying to cry midway through an attack. I grab a hold of her and lift her into a Fireman's carry. This isn't difficult. She is light, old and her body is going into shock at what just happened so there is no fight back. Once she is on my shoulders, I drop her over the balcony.
Within a few seconds, she is dead.

I throw my cup onto the concrete below and quickly move away from the balcony. I haven't time to waste. Next up is my date with the online prostitute, escort, or whatever you call them?
I whip off my glasses and put my blue Seattle Mariners baseball cap on with the matching blue hoodie from my bag. I walk out into the corridor and there she is. Standing a little over 5ft with long blonde hair and way too much makeup on and she is waiting, as instructed. I call her over and ask her to go into the bedroom and strip off. I explain that she is a gift for my mate who is getting married, and I want to provide him with one last hour of joy before he binds himself to the legal contract

of marriage and is stuck with the same woman until one of them dies. I hand her the agreed £300 and with that she winks and heads into the bedroom. As she closes the door, I hear a scream from outside. Winny has been found. I shout through to the slapper in the bedroom that I have to run upstairs to get my mate and I'll be back in a few minutes.

I walk out of the front door, head to the stairwell, and from the small windows I can already see people running towards the building. Once outside I follow the noise, the people, and there she is, Winny. In a horrible, crumpled heap on the floor.
A woman screams and says that she knows who this woman is. Whispers and words are exchanged between the onlookers.

The Police arrive along with an ambulance, and as they make their way through the crowd, they are told the name of the deceased and where she lived. An officer is deployed to head up to her flat on the 6th floor and secure the area.

A second Police car arrives, and the officers begin to push the crowd back. I can see at least four people with their phones out filming this event, so I stay firmly behind them. Last thing I need is to be spotted on camera during an extended episode of Crimewatch. As the crowd begins to break up, I take this as an excellent opportunity to vacate the area and head back to the

station. On the way I make a quick detour into Union Street where I dispose of my hat, hoodie and glasses, and put on my black hoodie and black beanie hat.
Ok, so not the most creative of costume changes, but I'm not going to whip out a peacock feather boa and big flashing glasses now am I.
Hope the prostitute is doing ok.

I'm on the train and looking out of the window. I don't know why because it's dark outside and bright inside. All I can see is the reflection of my face in the dirty glass and the tired, miserable faces of all the other passengers who are on this journey. It's a shame really as I enjoy the dark and looking up at the night sky and deep into the Solar System. Our Solar System. She has 8 daughters and one sun. She is bigger than we could ever imagine and so much more complex than we could ever understand, yet here we are. Fighting wars, polluting the waters, killing our people. The rich get richer as the poor dissolve into nothing. Famine and death run riot across our planet, and we look to the stars for inspiration. We raise our heads hoping something will ignite our compassion and deliver hope in one form or another, and from that we will march forward and succeed, but in truth, we do not. We are destructive, aggressive and arrogant. The seven deadly sins: pride, greed, wrath, envy, lust, gluttony and sloth, drive our very existence which exposes religion as a fraud, but we are all frauds.

Humanity has been harvesting what they can from this rock for hundreds of thousands of years, and this will never change. Stop thinking you're making a difference because you are not. Stop following your idols because they do not exist.

SIX : EXETER

I am so annoyed with myself right now. I got off the train at Exeter Central and just walked straight ahead. I had the bright idea of arriving at the train station masked up, so my face wasn't able to be recognised and, well, you know what I'm on about. I spent almost 3 hours on that pissing train wearing this fucking mask, sweating like a pregnant nun, and having to go to the toilet every 20 minutes to wipe salty forehead juice out of my eyes.

By the time I arrived in Exeter I was not in the right frame of mind and my original plan had long been forgotten.

I just had tunnel vision and walked straight down some road between the station and Exeter College I think it is, but I didn't get that far.

This road, path, back alley or whatever you want to call it is basically the service man's or staff entrance and car park to the shops and offices that surround this grey, forgotten area.

On my right as I stomped down this cut through, I spot a guy leaning against a wall in one of the empty car parks and without hesitation I went straight up to him and stabbed him right in the chest. I did it again and then twice more into his abdomen. When I launched my attack, he didn't fight back. He didn't say a single word. He didn't even scream. Maybe he was just glad

someone had finally put him out of his misery. Someone had finally come along and put an end to his useless existence. What sort of piece of shit was this anyway?
I dropped him onto the floor where he lay amongst his possessions. A dirty, heavily stained double duvet, a couple of carrier bags and just a load of random shit. Empty tins, toilet rolls and a picture of the Queen for some strange, creepy reason.

I sat down beside him and put the duvet over his blood-soaked body, and it was then that I noticed I had the same problem. Way too much of his blood is on my clothing. My light grey hoodie is ruined, and my jeans look just as bad. What the fuck am I doing here?
Not just here, sat on the floor with a dead smackhead, but here in Exeter.
Why am I here? Why have I just stabbed a man to death in broad daylight? This is a fucking mess, but let me ask you a question. What gets you through your worst days?
What makes you wake up in the morning?

This guy, fucking homeless smackhead guy, why does he wake up every day? Why does he, and every other homeless person living on the streets wake up in the morning? For what purpose? To just repeat the day before and achieve nothing.
I sit here next to you now and your journey in this life is over. I'm the alpha male and you're the prey, but they

loved you once. Maybe.

30 years ago, or however long ago it was, some woman got pregnant and for 9 months carried you around like a tumor until you got too big and had to be removed. What followed were your first steps toward death.
As you got older, every day got worse and you turned your back on life. You ended up living in this travelling dustbin of a home and spent your days waiting for the next day, until today.
I have ended your cycle, and you didn't even thank me. You, ungrateful shit!
I have done so much for you and this is how you repay me. With nothing. Nothing! Who the fuck do you think you are? I never asked you to be here, yet I did my best, but apparently that wasn't good enough. You ungrateful little shit!

I need to change my clothes.
I have a change of clothes in my bag, so that's not a problem. The problem is, what to do with this mess I've created?
I hide under the guy's duvet and get changed. It stinks and I can count at least 5 different stains, with blood being the obvious one, and the freshest. Once changed I cover the guy over best I can and head off back to the station as there has got to be a newsagent or something like that where I can grab some supplies. I am tempted to just bypass the shops and get straight on the train, but there is no way I can leave that mess behind.

I have to go to the shop. I need to fix this.

Hello, you ok?

Yes, I've just had a rough day and had a bit of a scrap with a guy in the pub.

I see. You look terrible.

Hmmm, thank you.

But you're ok?

Yes, I just want to grab some bits then head off home.

Ok, so anything else?

No that's it, thank you very much.

One bottle of cola, water, cigarettes, and chicken sandwich.

Yes, no sorry. Can I get a lighter as well. A decent one, thanks.

I couldn't find everything I needed here, so I walk further down the road and head into the local supermarket. Here I grab some petroleum jelly, crisps, face wipes, toilet roll and cotton wool. I hate buying toilet roll. People know at the moment of purchase that

I've run out and need to wipe my ass, or I ran out mid wipe and am walking around with bum cheeks caked in crap. Same when I was a kid and was made to go to the local shop and buy sanitary products for my mum. I found it so embarrassing and everyone in that shop, at that time knew that my mum was on the blob. At the age of twelve I'd happily go and buy her cigarettes or coffee but anything that was needed for things below the waist, then no thank you.

Anyway, shopping done, time to get back to that piece of human garbage I left in the alleyway and sit down. Halfway through my chicken sandwich, I notice what looks like a wallet underneath one of the bags. I grab a pair of my quilting gloves, slide them over my hands and pick up the wallet.

According to the store cards, the dead guy under the duvet might be Ash Rigby. Ash, well isn't that an appropriate name considering what I have planned. There isn't much else in the wallet except for the cards and a few receipts. For what? I don't care, but there is enough room in the wallet for me to leave something for them to find.

It's starting to get dark now and the train home leaves in 15 minutes. I'm amazed how no one has come anywhere near me since I've been sat here with Ash. I've had my back to the road the whole time I've been here and there is no CCTV so hopefully I haven't drawn any unwanted attention my way. Until now.

I pack my bag and say my last goodbyes to Ash. Now to set fire to the bastard using some petroleum jelly and a ball of cotton wool. I smear the jelly all over the ball and repeat the process a few times with a few balls and lay them on top of Ash. I leave the cigarettes, crisps and my mask and open the pack of toilet roll. One for me & one for Ash.
Now it's time to light a couple of these jelly balls and head off straight to the station. I reckon I have about sixty seconds until the fire erupts. Easily enough time to get to the station and disappear.
The toilet roll I've kept is for this terrible cold I suddenly have, so will keep the tissue against my face as I sneeze and cough my way through the station. Well, that's what it will look like to anyone that may pay attention, but I'm hoping that the upcoming nee-naw, nee-naw noises will keep everyone occupied and once my train arrives, I can get out of here.

As the train leaves the station, I feel strange. I don't know if I got away with this one or not. Was I too reckless? Did enough of Ash's body burn away and with it the evidence that I was ever there? I hope they find the wallet. I hid it under a nearby car so someone will pick it up.
Someone will see that I have ticked E off of my list. Someone will find the wallet. Twenty-one kills to go. I'm

tired, so I think I'll sleep.

That was the plan, but I can't sleep. I can't focus either. Not through my eyes, they work fine. I mean mentally. I can't focus. I'm all over the place and I don't know what I'm supposed to be thinking about. The train windows look itchy, I should scratch them, but I don't want to leave fingerprints. How can I remove my fingerprints? A pumice stone or pineapple juice perhaps, or cut them. Cut the skin on each finger so the skin becomes distorted so no accurate fingerprint can be found.
Why does this train have itchy windows? They are certainly dirty, maybe that's why they itch? Are train windows made of actual glass?
Maybe that's why they don't make coffins out of glass anymore because it makes the corpses itchy. They put Snow White in a glass coffin.

I remember we did Snow White once in our school play and I was the King. An Indian boy who had a white topknot that looked like a tiny chef hat played Snow White. He was the oldest in our year so gained instant respect and looking back he must have had a really laid-back approach to racism because you could not get away with that now. Casting an Indian boy to play Snow White based on the colour of his topknot. Maybe you could get away with it because of diversity and all that? Either way, it happened so let's move on. I remember I played the part of the King and even though I only had a few lines I can still remember some of what I said.

The first of which was me moaning about having to find a new Queen and it was all written in rhyme. I remember delivering my first lines and then the narrator took over as I paced the floor.

It wasn't easy for a King, to find himself this sort of thing.

Then there was other dialogue which I can't remember, but I remember the lead line to my final contribution to this play.
The King said with a shifty smile, to which I announced;
I'd like to give each one a trial.

This bit I remember so clearly.
We performed this play in front of a couple hundred kids and staff from the school, and after I delivered that line the room erupted in laughter. I can still see via the replays in my mind older kids and teachers laughing, clapping but I did not understand what was going on. I didn't get the joke. I thought trial was like a court thing. I enjoyed the attention, but the joke itself flew right over my innocent little head. I have since learnt that it was a joke about fucking many, many women which, looking back, is weird. I'm sure the whole play was packed with innuendo and dodgy comedy, but just from those two points alone–
Indian boy playing Snow White and the dirty misogynist approach to finding a new wife–I can see that we have come a long way in thirty years.

Go back even further than thirty years and it gets even worse. Snow White (not the Indian boy version) was apparently fourteen years old when the Prince (who was twice her age) fell in love with her. How this happened in the first place was even more unsettling. As the story goes, Snow White was poisoned by her stepmother and as a result, died. The seven miniature men she was living with didn't want to bury her, so they built a glass coffin to keep her in. Imagine the horror after a few months. There is no way they could have made that casket airtight so in time the elements would have affected the preservation of Snow White. Anyway, so she's dead and slowly decaying in this glass box for all to see when a Prince turns up and wants to have an intimate moment with the dead girl.

Hello dwarves.

Alright!

Yeah, who's in charge here?

Er, that'll be me.

Hello, my name is Prince Charming.

Nice to meet you, my name is Happy.

Happy?

Yes, it's because I'm happy.

Huh! So, I hear you've got a girl in a glass box, is that right?

We do, why?

Can I have a look?

Of course.

Thank you. Has she been dead long?

A few days now so she's on the turn.

What do you mean.

You know, changing colour and stiffening up.

Speaking of which. Do you mind if I...

Mind if you what?

Mind if I have a little kiss.

With her!

Yeah, is that ok?

Well, no not really. She's dead. Why do you want to kiss her?

Listen here tiny legs, I'm a Prince and I am telling you now that I am going to kiss her and if you refuse then you and all your goblin friends will not survive to see nightfall.

Ok, ok. Go ahead.

Thank you.

And so, the Prince kisses the dead girl, and she wakes up, but with severe brain damage due to the whole lack of oxygen and being dead situation. The Prince doesn't seem to mind so he carries her off to his castle and leaves the dwarves with nothing but an empty glass coffin. Snow White never spoke to her vertically challenged friends ever again, and one by one they faded away until there was just one remaining, Happy. In a house built for seven it became a lonely place.
A few months after Snow White left, a Huntsman was passing through the forest and decided to check in on his seven industrious friends. When he knocked on the door there was no reply. He knocked again, harder, and this time the door slowly opened. At that moment he fell to his knees and wept, as there in front of him, hanging from a wooden beam, was the tiny lifeless body

of the once Happy dwarf.

I like these old stories. Mad ideas that somehow work, but maybe that's just childhood memories talking. I mean, how could Pinocchio see where he was going if his eyes were made of wood!
Cinderella danced with the Prince even though she was wearing glass shoes.
Sleeping Beauty falls into a coma for 100 years and then a Prince wakes her with a kiss.
What the actual fuck is it with these Princes? Are they necrophiliac paedophiles or just really up for a challenge? Creepy bastards.

This may seem like pointless rambling, but this is good. This is keeping me occupied and calming me down. I can almost feel a sense of normality washing over me as the fury of today drips away.
Allowing my mind to just wander off in its own direction, and feed me ideas and theories to shit that doesn't need a theory written about it is a positive way of dealing with the reality of life. But, more often than not, these theories escalate into something unexpected and before I know it, they get out of hand. I start to question my own mind, my own judgement. Why am I thinking about young girls and pervy Royals? This sort of thing doesn't happen in the real world! Does it?

Although that isn't the story of Snow White it's the path I've taken in my retelling of this classic by the brothers

Grimm. When I share these thoughts in actual social interactions, I always get the same response;

You're weird (or) *I wish I had time to think up this sort of rubbish.*

It's not a question of having time. These things just pop in and take over, like today.
I wish I was there today to do things as I had planned, but rage took over. The side of me I hate so much, but it's a side of me I cannot live without.

Do conjoined twins really love each other?

I am getting so tired. My stop is a couple of minutes away and I need to get outside to the cold air. That should perk me up. My eyelids are so heavy. Every time my eyes close a loud noise wakes me up, but it's a loud noise that you will never hear. Only I can hear it. I don't want to hear it, but I can't control it. I can ignore it, but I will still hear it. I need to sleep.
I need some peace.

SEVEN : SILENCE

If we took a knee or held a minute silence for every atrocity that happens in this world we would never stand or talk again.
The world is a horrible place, yet we only see what we want to see. We are only told what we want to hear, and we only accept what our emotions can understand. Social media has given us a voice and we will be as loud as we can with no real-life consequence. We can troll, abuse, threaten and destroy anyone we want, whenever we want, all from the luxury of behind our screens.

We can hunt, groom and lust over what is not possible in the real world, but online it is all possible. I'm not talking about the deep web or the dark web; I'm talking about the worldwide web. These are sites me and you can access right now without raising suspicion. Zoophiles, paedophiles, extremists, terrorists and everything in between are free to roam the internet without limitations.

We take to the streets in our thousands to protest against homophobia, against police brutality, against anything we like. We feel we are part of a global movement, yet nothing moves. We are virtuous inhabitants of the ivory tower. Looking down, but never forward. Creating problems, not solutions.

We rip down statues and replace them with statues. We banish humour and scream for more diversity, yet there are still only 2 genders.

I see so much anger, aggression and hatred in our world that we have become our own depressing circus.
Send in the clowns! We can't, because they're already here. Face painted snowflakes stand screaming at the sky because opinions are offensive.
Feminists taking issue with how much space a man takes up on a tube yet ignores the true plight of women across the world, who are treated no better than dogs.
It would appear that the most privileged are indeed, the most oppressed.

I have grown to despise the people of the first world.
We are so vain, yet so afraid. Obsessed with ourselves yet refusing to admit the fact. Armchair activists applauding the latest trend to make us look and feel like we are making a difference. Yet all we are doing is following.
We spend all day being force fed lies and opinions disguised as lies and lies masquerading as opinions. I don't know what the truth is anymore. Fake news, deep fakes, fake media... I don't know who is in control. It is only since I came into incredible wealth that I have felt free. I am able to rise a few steps above everyone that I used to share the stairs with and now, if I want to, I can afford to take the lift whilst them below continue to struggle. It's not fair, but that's the way it has always

been and will always continue to be. The rich keep feasting as the poor go hungry.

But why do you care? You don't. I know that, you know that yet we continue to play this game.
Pass the parcel but the parcel is empty. A box of nothing wrapped up in newspaper displaying forgotten headlines that spark temporary outrage and create hashtags we can all get behind, until tomorrow.

Tomorrow we will have forgotten yesterday because there is a new parcel to play with, wrapped in paper that again reminds us that the world is shit. Corruption, famine, war, protests, fake news and everything else you can think of. We rip the paper to reveal the prize. There is no prize. The box remains empty, so we wait for tomorrow. Maybe then there will be something to celebrate? Maybe then we can break the silence and smile, talk or even cheer. Whilst we celebrate, we forget the stories written on the newspapers. The horror, the pain and the outrage. We forget for a brief moment the things that made us unhappy and wishing for a better life, because we have broken the silence.

In 1964 The Four Seasons recorded the song Silence is Golden, which I'm sure you know. High pitched male vocals at the ready,

Silence is golden, but my eyes still see.

You know the one. The term itself is from a much older proverb, speech is silver, and silence is golden. Either way, I do not agree.
Being silent for so long is what made me so ill. I wasn't in denial; it was just easier to keep quiet and pretend everything was okay. How does the saying go, it's okay not to be okay?

How are you, you okay?

No not really?

Oh, well that's okay.

What do you mean?

It's okay not to be okay.

Meaning what?

Although you're not feeling okay, that's okay. Meaning whatever is making you feel down will soon pass and everything will be okay again. So, it's okay not to be okay.

The truth is, it's not okay, not to be okay. It's not okay to be silent.
Silence is not golden, silence is the worst way of dealing with anything, especially mental health. I know this from personal experience. For me, being silent did

nothing for me, and here I am now. Talking to you, but you're not even here. Talking to myself about myself and getting more and more bored by the minute as I've heard this all before. But how can I if it's never been said? If I was silent then how have I heard it all before? Welcome to the inside of my mind. Whilst you're here, feel free to take whatever you want. I don't think I'll be needing it anymore. I don't own the contents; I'm just renting the space. Keeping it in order the best way I can until the owner returns. I think he's due back soon. He keeps threatening to evict me, but I always pay up when I need to and yes, I may have had a few accidents and caused a bit of damage but overall, the place is pretty much how he left it.

But why am I telling you this? What is the point, I mean you are just there, and I am just here, and this is just life, leading inevitably toward death. It's an endurance race. Whoever can last the longest wins, but no one really wins.

Let me tell you the short story of Stan and Albert.

Stan and Albert were both born on the same day, 2nd March 1951. They lived just a couple of streets away from each other in East Barnet. They both attended the same school and became great friends, right up until 1972 when Stan moved north to look for work. They tried to keep in touch but as the years passed life happened and in time, they forgot about each other.

In June 1979, Stan got married to the beautiful Rebecca

and between them had three boys. By the early 80s Stan was a senior partner in a ground-breaking new technology company and this put a real strain on his marriage.
1988 saw Stan and Rebecca file for divorce as she returned to Chelmsford to live with her parents.
Alberts life took a different direction. In 1974 he was arrested for the second time in as many years for robbery. This led to a twelve month jail term and when he was released, he went straight back to a life of crime. Between 1976 and 1982 Albert had spent more time locked up than he did on the streets. His life had become nothing more than a series of violent crimes and prison. By 1983 he had lost everything and was living wherever he could find shelter. Usually, in the dilapidated homes of drug dealers and prostitutes. The contacts he had made in the criminal underworld no longer wanted to know him and he was left with nothing. In December 1987 Albert was back inside for armed robbery and this time it carried with it an eight year sentence.

Stan returned to East Barnet in 1991 after he sold his part in the business to fund his return home. His father had died that year and he promised his mother he would be there for her. In 1993 he married again and worked at the local library for the following six years.
On the 14th of August 1999, Stan sadly died after a short battle against cancer.
At his graveside stood his three boys, his second wife,

their many friends and work colleagues. As the gathering broke and they said the last goodbyes, a member of the congregation noticed a familiar, yet well aged face. It was an old school friend. She was one of just a few people in attendance at another funeral that had happened earlier that morning. The funeral of Albert. It was a low-key affair as he was a vagrant, an ex-criminal who spent the last of his days drinking heavily and regretting every decision he had ever made. As the sun settled that day the stories of Stan and Albert came to an end.

Born on the same day, buried on the same day. Two completely different lives yet the end result is always the same, silence. In the endurance race that is life, Stan and Albert finished at the same time, yet Stan would be considered the winner because he had kids, married and contributed to society. Albert did nothing but steal and hurt people. Yet here they are, both dead and soon forgotten.

This is why life confuses me. Sometimes I want to live and be the absolute best me that I can, and then other times I see no purpose in living and think ending it today would be no different than ending it tomorrow. I can't seem to settle somewhere in the middle. All I want is to be happy, not just on the outside but also on the inside. Faking it is easy, being true to yourself is hard. It would help if I knew what I wanted out of life. Do you know what you want? Do you know what keeps you going. Are you Stan or are you Albert?

EIGHT : FOLKESTONE

We all know the story of Jack and the Beanstalk. Poor simpleton boy exchanges family cow for beans. His mother is furious, but the next day a magical beanstalk grew in the garden and reached up to the clouds. Without training or proper equipment, Jack climbs the beanstalk and partakes in a number of thefts. This all results in the giant that lives in the clouds being murdered by Jack as he tries to protect his property and belongings. This is a story that celebrates stupidity, theft and murder, but that is not what piqued my curiosity. I wanted to learn more about the weird man that gave Jack those beans. He is a minor character in the story, but one that makes the biggest impact. What was his agenda? Was he a disgruntled employee of the giant? Did he know what would happen if Jack went up the Beanstalk? Perhaps he was Jack's estranged father, looking for revenge against the boy's mother? Whoever he is, I want to know more. I want to know about him. I want a prequel to the story featuring this man and his motivation for apparent revenge. Sadly, I was never as lucky as Jack and never got access to a massive beanstalk. I didn't kill for my wealth, but now I kill thanks to my wealth.

My life wasn't always multiple property ownership, expensive masks and prostitutes. There were times in my life I would walk the streets looking for money.

Checking old phone boxes for whatever small change I could find. There were times in my life when I would steal from supermarkets so I could eat that day. There were also times when I've stolen just because I could, but now I have no need to steal. As I mentioned before, I have money. Lots and lots of money.
I attended a talk not too long ago & the wealthy guy who was stood at the front giving his speech was asked a question.

Even though you were rich, were you truly happy?

He predictably replied, no. Fuck off! How does the old saying go, *money doesn't buy you happiness*, like fuck it does. I'm the happiest I have ever been in my life since I've had money.
I am no longer living payday to payday. No longer getting threatening letters, phone calls and emails about how much money I owe loan providers, catalogues and the bank. No longer budgeting my meals for the week, and it feels amazing. I honestly recommend being wealthy. It makes you happy and makes you healthy.

Now these next few letters; G, H, I and J were always going to be tricky, but it's ok my invisible friend, because I'm a step ahead. During my year of planning I purchased a few properties, one in York YO30, one in Derby DE1 and one in Gloucester GL2. All really nice flats which I let to rent for 6 months so they don't stay

empty for too long. It would be weird if I suddenly rocked up one day with a set of keys and went into the flat a year after buying it. Rent them out first then once the tenants have moved on, I can then become the next tenant! Any neighbours that need to know will be told that I am an investor renting the property on a 6 month contract and that's all they will need to know. I hate nosey people, but they have their uses. They can provide an incredible alibi without even realising it. Feed them the right information at the right times and if questioned, that's the info they will turn to.
That may be true, or it may not be. I just have to play the long game and see what happens. As long as I feel in control then I am in control. This is my game to win, and I am in charge of the rules. Go ahead pick the colour of your counter, I'll go first.

Black.

My very first girlfriend was black. One of my best friends at little school was black.
I remember fondly that he used to steal toys and I would steal money from my mums' purse to pay for the stolen toys. I think I was around 8 years old? Problem is, one day we got caught. Probably because we were only 8 and not particularly smart when it came to criminal transactions. I remember my mum coming to the school and sitting with me and the teacher. I think they sat us in the playground on a wooden bench. My mum looked so beautiful with her long brown hair and calm

approach to the whole situation. I was so scared that I'd been caught, but she was firm with me, yet fair, and I knew from that day on, I had to get better at stealing. Instead of leaving finger dents in the sugar bowl when I used to eat the sugar, I would eat the sugar but then shake the bowl, so the sugar became flat. I would steal sweets from the corner shop. Chocolate bars from a different shop. Toys from toy shops and money from strangers.
I would walk out of my way to steal from shops I didn't know, and all of this would be for two reasons.

One: to prove to myself I could get away with it.

Two: because no one stopped me.

For a brief moment in time, I became someone. I was the kid that could steal pointless crap from shops. Pointless crap yes but after that day in the playground I have never been caught.
My black friend? I still see him about. We acknowledge each other with a smile and a nod of the head. No need to have a conversation as those days are far behind us. Enough reminiscing, it's time to get off the train.

Folkestone welcomes me with what I can only really describe as the least inspiring station exterior I've visited so far. It is basically one long grey rectangle of nothing with some blue on the end.

I don't want to dwell on this too long as this has the potential to turn into The Serial Killers Guide to English Train Stations, and that isn't what I set out to create. Perhaps, once I'm media famous, I could do a TV special and revisit some of my favourite locations. That would be fun.

The time is 1:13pm and my train out of here is at 1:54pm. From here, I'm heading to my pad in Gloucester for a few nights. The journey will be straightforward enough. A couple of changes in London along the way and by the time I get to Gloucester it will be early evening.

As I walk toward the public toilets at Radnor Park it's at this point, I realise something. I'm only 5 letters in, but every murder I've committed up to this point has been in close proximity to the train station and the same applies here. I haven't exactly gone out of my way each time. Andover, Basingstoke, Cambridge, Doncaster, Exeter and now here have all been within walking distance from the station. Fuck!
A sudden wave of panic sweeps over me but I can't let this knock me off track. I remind myself to enjoy the feeling. Enjoy the sense of panic and stress. These are real emotions and like relief and euphoria, they need to be enjoyed. I repeat this time and time again along with my breathing.

6. 6. 6.

Without hesitation, I enter the public toilets and stand in the cubicle and wait. Radnor Park is massive and there are enough people about that I shouldn't be waiting too long.

I'm using a hammer again today. I am planning to replicate my first attack in Andover and create a bit of a link between that attack and this. The Hammer Toilet Killer sounds awful, but it's a good start in terms of getting me noticed and on people's radars. Hopefully then some bright spark at Police HQ will piece together the puzzle and realise that there are more deaths.

You see, at each location I have left a single page from a printed alphabet book that corresponds with the first letter of the place name. It's like one of those baby books that helps them with the alphabet. A is for Apple; B is for Ball and, you know how the rest of it goes. Once they piece all that together I reckon I'll be up to around the letter P, then the game of cat and mouse can begin.

Hush, someone has come in and standing at the urinal. Time to make an appearance. I flush the toilet to create some noise and step out of the cubicle. There is a guy, probably my height, slim, short dark hair. Just a generic bloke really. He stands there with his back to me, happily pissing and humming to himself. I take a swing at his head and the force of the blow smashes his forehead into the ceramic tiles in front of him. I swing at him again and he goes down. I am about the take a third swing at him, but I'm frozen. A kid is standing there, staring at me. This kid must be no more than 7 years old. Maybe this is his Dad? We make eye contact and as we do, I strike the guy one last time. The kid jumps as the hammer makes contact with the skull of the now dead man.

Maintaining eye contact, I stand tall and do something that I hope I will not regret in the future. I reach into my jacket inside pocket and pull out a £10 note. This particular note has been sat in my pocket since Andover and I have scribbled the word lucky onto it. The idea behind it was that I would give this to someone who, would get a free pass. A chance to continue living. Well done little boy, today is your lucky day.
Once I put the hammer back in my bag, I hand the £10 note to the boy and with the other hand I press my finger against my lips in a shushing motion. The boy takes the note from me as I walk past him and straight out of the door. It's 1:46pm. The train departs in 8 minutes.

Why did that kid have to walk in?
Why did that kid have to walk in?

I can't stop repeating the question over and over in my head. I hope he's ok. I mean, it's not my problem and

I'm never going to see him again, so why should I care if he's ok or not?
I think his name is Aiden Jones or, Andre Jeans? The note I gave the boy had the serial number AJ45845406. The AJ must be his or his Dads initials and the numbers, all added together come to 36. So, the guy I killed must be 36 years old and the boy must be 9 (3+6). Mrs. Jones must have been in the park as well. Probably changing the baby. As she was doing that the man walked to the toilet and the boy, after arguing with his Mum about needing to have a piss or not must have run after his Dad a minute or so later.
Mr. Jones is now dead, Aiden returns to his Mum and by the time she pieces everything together, I am long gone. Now that's 2 kids growing up without a father. I'll be honest, this has shaken me a bit. Why did he have to walk in!

It is approaching midnight and I'm pouring the last drops of Cabernet Sauvignon into my glass. The view from my window isn't much, but at least it's dark and more importantly, quiet. I stand on my balcony and feel a sense of guilt. I thought I killed guilt years ago, but it would appear not. Why did the kid have to come in after his Dad?

Maybe he didn't.

What?

Maybe, he didn't. Maybe that was just a kid who needed to use the toilet.

Yeah but why would he have come in after the dead man?

Well, if the dead man walked in first, then the kid had no choice but to follow after.

What about the initials and numbers on the bank note?

What if the initials had been BB?

But they weren't.

What if the numbers were 14020141? That adds up to 13.

But they were not the numbers.

By your logic the name would be something like Billy Brunsdon who is a thirteen year old man and has a four year old son.

You just don't get it do you. That isn't the case. He was given the note with the..

I know what he was given, I was there, but I'm telling you the moment has gone. Those digits and letters on the note do not mean anything...

In a burst of rage, I throw my glass against the wall. Red wine and glass shards now occupy that particular corner of my living room.

Stay out of my head! You don't know me. You don't own me.

I walk away from the balcony not knowing what is going on. The numbers, the letters, the noise. It's so quiet yet I can't hear myself think.
Shut up! Shut up! **SHUT UP!!**

In the kitchen I open another bottle of red but this time I have no need for a glass. I'm drinking straight from the bottle. This is the quickest way to silence that voice.

Who is Ash Rigby?
Who is Aiden Jones?
Are they real or fantasy?
That I do not know.

NINE : GLOUCESTER

You lay in a hospital bed. Crisp white sheets, white pillowcases, and a white blanket. You've always preferred a light blue or green colour scheme when it comes to the interior decoration of your private chambers, but today it is not your choice. It hasn't been your choice for the past 19 days as you've been laying here, waiting to die.
Your eyes open and the first face you see is that of your daughter. She is as beautiful as the day she was born. She has always been your little girl and will forever be. Her hair isn't as blonde as it once was and her choice in partners hasn't always been what you would consider acceptable, yet here she stands, on your left-hand side, smiling. Through wet, tired eyes, she is still smiling.
To your right is your youngest son. An adult to everyone else, but in your eyes still a child. You can still see the mischief within him and the ever so subtle smirk across his top lip. He will never show his emotions yet, he hasn't let go of your hand now for the past hour.

Standing in the far corner of the room is another one of your boys. He is struggling with what is happening and walks out of the room. He's always been one to shy away from difficult situations. Is this the last time you will ever see him? You hope not. You hope for one more terrible joke, one more hug, one more smile, but it's too late, he's gone. The door swings wildly behind him as your eldest enters the room with his wife. They have been with you for the past year as your health has deteriorated. Watching you every day, helping you stay alive, but it just became too much and here you are. In the hospital, in this bed, with white sheets.

You look up at the clock. The thin second hand is spinning fast. Way too fast in fact. You try to focus on the clock face and count along with the seconds as they whizz by, but it's impossible. The hands become blurred as time becomes nothing more than a gesture. You close your eyes and take in a painful last breath. As you exhale, you open your eyes and look at your family one last time.
You know they are there, but you can't see them. You can't feel their hands on your hands or hear their words as they speak. In your mind you shout so loud that you love them, every one of them. They can't hear you and they will never hear from you again. There is no more breath. Your lungs are emptying, and everything is shutting down. As your eyelids drop one last time, you can see a light. A bright, welcoming light in the distance. Not too far away, but far away enough that you will have to leave now to make it in time. You need to separate your spiritual self from your physical body so you can live a life of eternal happiness in heaven. The light is the way, this is your salvation.

Three seconds pass and they declare you officially dead. Within 20 minutes the room is empty and you are alone, with your white sheets, white pillowcases and white blanket.

Or, another way of looking at this would be; There is no more breath. Your lungs are emptying, and everything is shutting down. As your eyelids drop one last time, you see and feel nothing. You whisper to yourself and admit that you're scared, cold and alone. What follows is darkness. Eternal darkness and nothing. No feelings, no emotions, no light. No heaven, no hell. Nothing. You become dust. Carried around in a jar, acting as a ceramic reminder that you are dead.

I've been in my apartment now for five days and I'm calm. I didn't stop drinking for 2 days and it's only today I'm starting to feel good, and by good, I mean alive. You see, I ordered something online a couple of weeks ago and it arrived during my 2 day bender and the idea of suicide crossed my mind on more than one occasion, but as you can tell, I am still here.

What I ordered was a murder mystery classic from the realms of Miss Marple and Poirot, and that is cyanide. 250ml of it in liquid form and the package that arrived today is for various sized syringes plus a high quality 23-gauge needle. I worked out the conversions of 1.5mg of poison per kg of body weight so I have more than enough to get this done. I thought it would be good to take a break from the hammer and knife attacks plus if someone links Andover and Folkestone together as the

Toilet Hammer Attacks then this will no doubt throw them off the scent a little.
Tomorrow I will take a walk to the top end of Southgate Street which is about 20 minutes away from my apartment and select my prey. From there I'll head back to my apartment and lay low for a couple of days before heading back down to Hampshire.

Ok, so I've just spent 2 hours trying to pierce the needle of the syringe into a bullseye I've scribbled onto a cushion, but I can't do it. I've tried a couple of mask variations, but each of them appears to have limited vision once my head is above my hands so I can't see where the needle point is going. Think I may have to scrap the mask idea for tomorrow, especially as I need this to work first time. Stabbing is different. It can be a frenzied attack and the result will be death, but this, this is a one shot and one shot only attempt. With that in mind, I'm going to go with sunglasses and a baseball cap. I think tomorrow I'll be a Boston Red Sox fan. For now, time to head off to bed for some light reading about Nazis.

Did you know...
Cyanide or Suicide Pills were first developed by the British and American secret services during World War 2. These pills were filled with highly toxic potassium cyanide and hidden inside a fake tooth. They distributed these amongst special agents who had missions behind enemy lines, and if the mission was compromised in any

way, they would crush the fake tooth in order to digest the poison. Also, if the tooth were to be swallowed accidently, it would just pass through the body with no ill effects. There are many links to some high profile Nazis who took their own lives using a cyanide pill including Herman Goering, Heinrich Himmler and Eva Braun. It has even been suggested that Hitler's closest associate, Joseph Goebbels, had used cyanide to murder his own children before taking his own life.

It's 6:15am and I'm wide awake and ready to go. Annoying really as I didn't plan on venturing outside until 2pm once the lunchtime rush was over, but I might just head out early instead.

It's 9:15am and I've left my apartment. I just couldn't do it. I just couldn't sit down and relax for a few hours. At least I can take a slow walk to Southgate Street and enjoy the fresh morning air. Well, as fresh as it can be when walking alongside a busy road for most of the journey. It's cool though. Every person I walk past I feel a sense of power, a sense of ownership over their lives. With a swift move of my hand, I can end their lives in seconds. However, I will stick to the plan and see what happens when I get to Southgate Street.
Cyanide, not as difficult to get hold of as you would imagine. The dark web, deep net or whatever you want to call it, basically the stuff you can't find via your regular search engines, is host to plenty of sites to get stuff like this. I got myself a gun once, but that's another

story. I didn't fire it, I just used it as a tool in a little game I was playing. I like games. Although having the gun in my hand did bring on a rush of pro-suicide ideas. It would be so easy, so quick, but then I think I've read stories of people who have tried to shoot their heads off and some how survived. How rubbish would that be. Waking up after a dramatic suicide attempt only to find out you survived, and to makes things worse, you now only have half a head. Forever on medication and forever regretting your decision. Probably wouldn't be able to wear a hat properly either. Sad times.

Something is kicking off outside of the mini supermarket. I walk with added haste toward what appears to be an argument and shoving match between a few guys and some mouthy bitch who is just screaming at all of them. Why do they do that? Floating, hanging around the outside of an argument, just screaming. They say it's wrong to hit a woman. It's ok to inject cyanide into her though, isn't it? Problem is I am the wrong side of the scuffle so can't get to her unless I make an obvious move toward her and there will no doubt be CCTV coverage or at least some kind of PCSO intervention soon. I'll stay here, behind the guy who looks as though they have accused him of shoplifting. He is arguing with a member of staff and another random bloke. I have no idea what is going on, but I'm enjoying it.

The more I look at this woman, the more curious I become. She is ugly. Not physically ugly, just ugly. Her attitude and her character make her utterly repulsive, but this repulsion does not extend to the men in her life. No matter who they are, I bet she's fucked them all. After she sucked her schoolteacher off at the age of 12, she realised that her mouth, her vagina and her anus were what would get her what she wanted in life. She has never worked for anything, and she believes she has everything she could ever need, but I would love to be the one to give her something she has yet to experience. I would take her and fuck her in a way she has never been fucked before. I would drill her full of new holes and penetrate her that way. I would plant a pickaxe into her spine, mount her and fuck her. Fill her with my fluid as it becomes one with her own. Ugly bitch.

My syringe is ready as I wait for the right moment, and the right moment has just presented itself. The random guy pushes the shoplifter guy into me and as he does so the needle goes straight into his lower back. The dirty Swiss cheese girl swings an open hand at the shoplifter, and he goes down. Motionless. Still. By this point, I have slid the needle back up my sleeve and taken a few steps back. The member of staff jumps in but not before the woman has swung a boot at the guy's head.
She looks thrilled with herself,

I knocked him the fuck out.

Yes, yes you did. Well done.

The pretend Police have arrived as expected and ask people to step back so they can deal with the situation. That's not a problem I need to head back to my apartment and have lunch.

You know what; I didn't enjoy doing that. It felt lazy, like I had taken the easy option. There's no proper human to human contact. No moment of looking deep into the eyes and seeing if they know that death is on its way. Maybe I ordered too much cyanide, I still have plenty left. I guess I could use it again at the back end of the alphabet, Wrexham, York or wherever. York could work as I have a property there so it would pretty much just be a repeat of today, or would that be too obvious? I could pour the rest of the poison into the water supply or put it in a giant water pistol and go on a fun and colourful killing spree during the height of summer. Can you imagine that?
People sat happily in a park and I'm walking about squirting them with a homemade water/cyanide solution. At first it would be fun, I mean no one minds getting sprayed on during the height of summer, but what would the cyanide do to the skin? Maybe I'd have to spray it into their mouths to get a fatal reaction? Well, let's wait and see shall we. For now, I'm done and going to have some food, a couple of beers and watch the film Warriors. It's one of my favourite movies from

my childhood along with the original Robocop film, Rambo, Commando and Die Hard. I guess as a kid I should have been watching soppy Disney films or something, but I didn’t and here we are and to be honest, I’d take Bruce Willis or Arnie over Mickey Mouse every time.

TEN : RESURRECTION

Two outcomes are guaranteed with suicide. You either die or you don't. Me? I died.
Well the old me died. The new me who you know as Kane, is perfectly fine and speaking to you now. Problem is, I'm not using my resurrection, my second chance, as an opportunity to inspire but instead as an opportunity to right the wrongs that have plagued me all my life. Those wrongs? Those wrongs are you.

Let's back track a few years and start from there.

Once upon a time... I started working for a large retail company as a member of their security team, which in itself was a bit of a joke as I did not cut a particularly intimidating figure. The reason I got the job was I had worked at a number of venues and events such as Royal Ascot, Twickenham, Wembley Stadium and a number of lives shows in and around the London area. Thanks to that line of work I've been able to see some of the greats play live, up close, and for free!
Bon Jovi, Red Hot Chili Peppers, The Prodigy, Metallica, Slipknot, Linkin Park, Cliff Richard and Celine Dion.
Ok, the last couple I listed were actually nothing but a fucking chore but at least I was getting paid to be there. I also worked at some mad little jazz and folk festivals as well. They were great fun. Do fuck all work all day and

then nick stuff from the bar when everyone was clearing down.
I remember at one of these little festivals me and a couple of the other guys managed to steal a load of red wine boxes and piled them into our getaway car. Problem was, the fat lad who was driving didn't want us using his car as a place to store our treasures so we had to do it without him knowing. Obviously he realised what was going on once he arrived to drive home, but by then it was too late.

All in all there were twelve of us working this gig and all split between three cars. That worked out well as we could all fit nicely in between the stolen boxes of vino.

It was a forty mile journey back home and on the way the most beautiful thing happened. One of the wine boxes in the fat lads car split and covered the back seat in a crimson blanket of stink. Oh, did I mention it was actually his mums car. We all pulled into a service station where he had a proper meltdown.

What am I going to do?

Whimpering like a bloated baby who had just shat himself, it was the best part of the whole day.
Someone did try to clean it by pouring water all over the back seats but that somehow made things worse.

The boxes of wine were then removed from the whimpering boys car and split evenly between the remaining cars and thinking back, I don't think he ever worked with us again.

I have so many of these stories from my security days, like the time I was tossed off in a bin bag, or the time Rod Stewart laughed at me. Or how about the time I had the chance to assassinate Prince William!
No, I think my favourite was when I refused a well-known TV actress access to a backstage party because she was wearing the wrong-coloured wristband.
It's not a great story but it was then that I realized I had power.
This skinny little prick from Southampton has power over people, and it felt amazing.
With great power comes great asshole!
Ok I know that's not the saying and I don't even think it makes sense but that is exactly what happened. I became a massive asshole.

I would work festivals and confiscate drugs. Check the shoes, hats, tampons. I had the right to search and soon learnt the sneaky little hiding places that everyone used. It became very clear to members of the security team that I enjoyed this side of the job, and the more obnoxious I became, the better the jobs I was offered. No more working the fences at small events, I was working VIP areas at Wembley, Executive Boxes at a couple of English football clubs and mingling with posh knobs in the Winners Circle at Goodwood. The pay hadn't really improved but my ego was happy.

In time ownership of the security business changed hands and I did not get on with the new boss. The only real reason being was that he wanted me to do overnight static security. Fuck that! I'm not spending ten hours in my own company with nothing but a torch to keep me entertained. The reason he wanted me off of the high profiles jobs and into the static work was because I wasn't a fat fuck. You see he believed that a *security officer* had to present in a certain way and my 34" waist fell way short of the mark.
Maybe the fat lad with the red wine smelling car got the last laugh after all.

Shooting forward 4-5 months or so and I landed this security job within retail and was placed to work alongside a couple of old pros who did not take shit off anyone. It was great working with them but if truth be told. I wasn't cut out for this job.

I made it clear to my boss on more than one occasion that I wanted to move up within the company into a more managerial role but that wasn't going to happen anytime soon.

Being allowed access to the camera room was a step in the right direction. I mean, it got me out of being on the

shop floor and gave me a chance to just waste my time perving on customers.
Summertime was fantastic. It never took too long before a well-endowed female would walk in, and thanks to the wonders of modern technology, I was able to invisibly follow her around the store, staring at her tits.
Maybe she was a shoplifter? A thief? Maybe she was but I wasn't interested in that.
We had one woman who used to come in who was so exposed that it drove other members of the security team up to the camera room just to gawp at her massive knockers.
Knockers, is that an acceptable word to use to describe a pair of tits?
If not, what would you prefer? Boobs, Bristols, Hooters, Bazookas, Baps, Norks, Melons, Bongos, Juggs, Chubby Chest Cheeks, Gazongas, Traffic Stoppers, Shirt Potatoes, Party Pillows., Dinosaur Eggs, Lady Bubbles or perhaps we could just call them The Smother Brothers?
Either way, I wasn't alone when it came to enjoying the pleasures of the flesh, albeit via an instore security camera.

Eventually summer dragged into autumn, and autumn into winter which means more clothes were worn and the idea of working the camera room became a major bore. But fear not, change was on the way and it came in the form of a step up into a team leader role. It was in the cash office which was weird, but a move up is a move up. It also gave me access to a steady stream of cash. I'll explain.

Thanks to my time in security, I knew the location of every camera in the store and with that, every blind spot. I knew the time schedules of when the cameras were manned and when they weren't. At home I had a map of the stores camera positions and how effective each one was.
I sketched out the area within the cash office where I knew the cameras could see and where they couldn't. I had everything in place, this was going to be so much fun.

It took me a couple of weeks to find my feet in this new vocation but once I had settled in, and the four ladies I worked alongside accepted me, I set my plan in motion.

On any given day there would be an average of 10 till banks active and with that 15-20 different employees would use these. Some working short 4 hour shifts, others doing a full day. Being in the cash office I had access to every tube that would shoot through the tunnel from the shop floor. All I had to do was unscrew the top of the tube and the notes would just fall out onto the table top, but sometimes into my pocket, or shoe, or jacket sleeve.

How? Easy! I would position myself directly under one of the cameras which was situated in the corner of the

office, therefore having my back to the camera on the opposite side.
I knew the camera above my head couldn't see me, except for maybe the top of my scalp but could certainly not see my hands.

Overseeing the cash office gave me the power to determine when the staff would have their lunch and tea breaks. My direct line-manager was never in the office as she had too much to deal with out on the shop floor, especially now as I was in the zone and had picked my target.
Till number 8 was used by some kid whose name I can't remember so for the sake of this story let's call him Steve.
All I had to so was wait for Steve to start his shift and as soon as his tubes started popping into my hands, I would begin harvesting the takings.
One technique I employed was to roll up and slide a £20 up into my jacket sleeve then fake a yawn. This way I was able to raise my arm a little higher and push the note under the strap I was wearing. I would also hide notes in my shoes, once they had fallen off the desk, as well as just simply slip them into my trouser or jacket pocket. Leaning over to grab a calculator or a pen was another great way to make things disappear.

After a while I would excuse myself, head across the shop floor, into the back staff area and up onto the toilets where I would retrieve the notes from their

various hiding places. I would them slip them into my wallet because that's where they've always been, of course.
These things were never checked before I started my shift because I was trusted. I mean, I used to work on security so I must be trustworthy.

A few weeks later Steve was put under investigation and subsequently fired. Oopsy! I would say I stopped after this, but I didn't.
I was never walking out the store with hundreds, but that extra £20 - £60 a day I was walking home with allowed me to make sure I was eating and drinking well every night, but it made me feel like I was winning this little game I had created. As I said before, I like games.

INTRODUCING SATAN

Satan is simply a word that means the adversary, or the opposition, or the accuser. It doesn't necessarily mean evil or brutality, or cruelty. It simply means the dissenter.

-Anton LaVey

At this point in my life I became a Satanist and still to this day hold the core beliefs of the Nine Satanic Statements which appear in the Satanic Bible.

1. Satan represents indulgence instead of abstinence!
2. Satan represents vital existence instead of spiritual pipe dreams.
3. Satan represents undefiled wisdom instead of hypocritical self-deceit.
4. Satan represents kindness to those who deserve it instead of love wasted on ingrates.
5. Satan represents vengeance instead of turning the other cheek.
6. Satan represents responsibility to the responsible instead of concern for psychic vampires.
7. Satan represents man as just another animal, sometimes betters, more often worse than those that walk on all-fours, who, because of his 'divine spiritual and intellectual development' has become the most vicious animal of all.
8. Satan represents all of the so-called sins, as they all lead to physical, mental, or emotional gratification.
9. Satan has been the nest friend the church has ever had, as He has kept it in business all these years.

I would read The Satanic Bible each and every night, and when I reached the last page, I would start again. Within a few months of living like this, things became more bizarre than they already were.

I managed to steal enough money from my job to walk away from it. I didn't tell them, I just didn't turn up ever again.
I don't know what happened to the other people that ended up under investigation for theft but obviously they were innocent, even poor Steve, but I needed the money. Wait, no I didn't. I didn't NEED the money, I WANTED it. I wanted the money so I took it.
I now had no job and only enough money left over to pay the rent on my flat for one more month. This wasn't a concern. What ever plot I had, I'd lost it and everything kind of went to shit soon after.

On an average evening I would crack open a couple of cans of lager followed by a bottle of red wine.
After that I would finish whatever was laying around, be it more lager, cider or another bottle of red.
By this point I was ready to indulge in a little bit of blade play. Perhaps you would be more comfortable calling it self-harm? There were many different ways I would arouse my skin in preparation for the inevitable attack, but I found wine and extreme heavy metal music worked best.

I would go out looking for fights and more often that not would fail, but when the violence did come my way, I got the living shit kicked out of me.

I would destroy property, get arrested. Spend the night locked up, go home, sleep, wake up drink and start the process all over again.

Eventually, money was beginning to run low so I decided to stay home more often. To make my evenings more bearable I constructed an alter and adorned it with various Satanic trinkets. I would now spend my evenings sitting cross legged in front of the alter practicing various Satanic rituals, listening to Satanic black metal and sipping red wine. Indulgence at the highest level.

Cutting was still included in my activities but now it had become an addiction. No longer a precursor for violence, instead it was on par with drinking. It became a necessity. I still carry the scars and the oddest one I have to explain is the large one across my stomach. It is about 6 inches long and was created during sex with someone. That someone is, well she is. That someone is dead to me now, I think.

I've drawn on a horse!
I'll explain.
After downing a bottle of the red stuff I felt like going for a walk so I went out and took a couple of sharpie pens with me. I never planned to unleash my art on a living creature but it happened. I can't remember what I doodled on the horse but I do remember finding the whole thing very therapeutic, until the horse got pissed

off with me. It started doing that grunting noise and even though he was tied up I knew it was time for me to leave. One swift kick in the knackers from one of those and it's game over. Out of interest, what is the largest animal you've ever drawn on?

This cycle of crazy just kept on going and going. Cutting, drinking, fighting, stealing, and praying to the almighty Satan that he release me from the world that I feel I no longer belong to.
I would imagine the conversation with Him was real. I promised that if He helped remove me from this world then in return, I would bring a rage and intelligence unmatched by any of His current generals. I would stand shoulder to shoulder with his greatest leaders and prepare the demons for a war against the heavens.

He accepted my proposal but before I went, I wrote one last poem.

Voice and words
Mumbled and jumbled
As clear as day
Sounds as sharp as a pin
The physical me
Seen in the mirror
Beyond my eyes
Is unimaginable noise

I bend down to Satan and pray to his name
I stab out the eyes of my enemies
The hot candle wax drips and spells out your name
I carve in my chest to pass on the blame

Voice and words
Angry and mocking
Are said everyday
As sharp as a pin
The physical me
Gets battered and broken
Fighting again
To unimaginable noise

I bend down to Satan and wonder if he's there
Read every page of your bible
I stagger each night with blood on my fingers
Ready for war as I fight all alone

I cry to the alter
Made of candles and wine
My curtains twitch
As the flame flickers out
In silence, I feel you
Your hand, cold to touch
You whisper, I hear
It's now time to jump

My memories of what happened that night are disjointed at best. All I can recall is it was dark and past midnight. How many minutes past midnight, I have no idea.

I was walking across the Itchen Bridge in Southampton and as I reached the middle, I knew it was time. Time to say goodbye. All that stood between me and forever darkness was a 4-foot concrete wall. This was never going to stop me.

Past the wall was a 90 foot drop into the freezing water below. The bridge itself has witnessed more than 200 (alleged) suicides since it opened in 1977, so at least I've picked a popular spot.

I rest my hand on the metal bar that runs along the wall.

I can hear Him calling me.

It's time.

When I woke I was not alone.
I was laying in a bed, in a room I did not recognise, then it dawned on me. I was in hospital.
My left arm was in a plaster and my right hand had a tube coming out of it.
What the fuck happened?
I try to get out of bed but was told to stay put by the over friendly nurse. Not nice genuine friendly but that fake *I'm paid to be friendly* type of attitude.
I waited almost an hour to be seen by the doctor who explained to me I was involved in a traffic accident and suffered a concussion and a fractured radius.

The conclusion drawn was that I was drunk and wandered out into traffic. Got clipped by a car and then submitted to hospital. Not by the driver of the car that hit me, someone else.

A couple more hours passed and I decided it was time for me to leave. I felt well enough but I was not allowed to do so without supervision due to the head injury. Great! Now what do I do, I have no one.

I sat back down on the hospital bed. I wonder how many have died in this very bed? How much blood, piss and other bodily secretions have been spilt by someone laying, convulsing in this very bed. Nasty, dirty places.

I've managed to construct a lie in my head about someone picking me up soon so I can get out of here but before I could say anything the nurse with the fake happy face informs me that they've managed to contact my father who will be here within the next couple of hours to collect me.

My father? Shit. This isn't good.

ELEVEN : HEREFORD

Do you mind if I sit here?

No, not at all.

I move my bag off of the table so the guy can sit down opposite me on the train. After a few minutes he makes himself comfortable and pulls out his laptop and can of coffee from his stupid brown leather bag. He's annoying me already.

Busy?

Pardon.

Just asking if you're busy. You look like you're setting up your office on this small table.

Sorry is that a problem.

No, no. You working?

Yeah afraid so.

What do you do?

I'm a journalist.

A what?

Journalist.

Ah, journalist. How do you spell that again? Is it C, U, N… I forget the last of that.

Sorry but what is that supposed to mean?

Who do you work for? One of the big nationals?

That's none of your business.

Who?

I'm freelance if you must know.

So, you scurry inside other people's dustbins trying to find a vague piece of information that you can turn into a headline and sell to the highest bidder.

No, it's nothing like that.

Fuck off.

What's your problem mate?

You are vermin. No, sorry that's really rude of me. I love rats and squirrels. You wish you were vermin. You are scum. People like you don't fucking care.

Erm, I'm sorry what?

You're not sorry. The lives that people like you have ruined. Rooting through the social media posts of the deceased in an attempt to spice up the story. Ignoring the feelings of grieving families. Pissing kerosene onto bonfires hoping it will ignite and erupt into the flames of war. Forcing your political agenda by hiding the truth and being the best friend to whatever bandwagon rolls into town.

You are out of order mate.

Shut up. You hunt with your cameras and kill with your words. You are scum.

With this the journo stands up and attempts to move on. I grab his arm and look straight into his shitty little face.

People like you are why this country is such a fucking mess. Reporting nothing but lies to support hidden agendas and to appease certain minorities. You wouldn't know the truth if it raped you and bit your fucking tiny cock off.
Now fuck off.

I release his arm and he vacates the carriage, carrying with him his laptop and his ugly brown bag. I stay sat down, staring at the empty seat. This virus that infected my space has pissed me right off. I hate weakness and journalists fit snugly into that category. You will often find them hiding behind someone else's money or someone else's name and when challenged they crumble. Too afraid to be honest. Too afraid to ask the right questions to get an answer that everyone will understand. Imagine if for 24 hours everyone told the truth. Wouldn't the world just become a better place? Not straight away because of the inevitable backlash against governments and organised religion, but in time, the world would become united because we all knew that for 24 hours no one lied.

Excuse me, sir.

I take a deep breath. How dare he interrupt my thinking time! This had better be important.

Sir, hello excuse me.

What me, I've already shown you my ticket.

Yes sir, no this is about an incident that took place here.

Sorry you're going to have to explain in more detail what exactly you're on about.

It has been reported that you have been acting aggressively towards another passenger on this train.

Right.

Is this correct sir?

Do you see anyone sat with me? Who have I been aggressive toward?

Sir, it has been suggested that you verbally and physically attacked another passenger.

Suggested?

Sorry.

You said suggested. You saying the word suggested, suggests to me you're just hoping for me to admit to something because... The CCTV doesn't work does it.

Can we stick to the matter at hand.

No, no, no. That camera above your head and the one at the back of the carriage, they don't work do they.

Sir ,we just need to clarify what happened before we pull into Newport station. British Transport Police have been informed of the incident and if required will intervene...

Hang on. Hang on one minute. Was this complaint from a guy, short brown hair, glasses, wearing a grey blazer, jeans and carrying a brown holdall.

That does…

Ah ha, the bastard.

Excuse me.

Not you. My other half. We had a bit of an argument as we are trying to get our relationship back on track after he cheated on me and yes, I'll honest I have a bit of a temper, but we are trying to work this out. A bit of space right now is good for us. Believe me, by tonight he will be riding me like a…

Ok sir you need not say anymore. There are other people on the train who do not need to hear about your personal life.

That's ok, sorry. Also, I apologise for being so rude. Like I said, it's been a tense couple of weeks. I hope you understand.

But the complaint needs…

If you want, I can go and speak to Glynn now and together we can just get this sorted, but I can't guarantee it will be amicable. That's why we need some space right now.

Erm, that's ok sir. I'm sure you two will work it out once you get to Newport. Sorry to bother you.

That was close! I am happy to argue with a lowly train guard, but I can't risk drawing attention to myself from any kind of Police, even the BTP.

We arrive at Newport and there is no sign of the BTP so that's good. I have about 20 minutes before the next train to Hereford, so I just find an empty bench to sit on and wait.

I have your picture.

I look up and the journo from the train walks past me grinning, holding his phone.

I have your face. Fuck you.

I can't react as the platform is busy so all I can do is stare at this bag of shit as he walks away. Has he really taken my photo? SHIT! This is why I have masks! Why am I not wearing one? FUCK. Nothing I can do, but maybe the prick will get hit by a bus in the next few minutes. He deserves it.

Arriving at Hereford station I turn right and head down what can only be described as an industrial estate back alley, yet it has a bowling alley, arcade or some type of fun building here. Looks nice enough I suppose and is perfect if you want a last-minute game of bowling before you jump on the train, but that's not why I'm here. I find a quiet spot in the empty car park, which is behind the bowling place and next to, I don't know what that is and to be honest; I don't care. I don't have time for sightseeing. It's quiet so I can get changed, mask up and get on with my task. Mask and Task. I like that, if I expand my operation that would be the company name.

Back to today, I am an older Asian gentleman, and this mask is lush. Add a surgical protective face mask, which seems to be acceptable attire for Asians based in the UK, and I look pretty good.
Why do so many Asians in the UK wear these face coverings? Seems to be more the younger generation. Do they know something we don't? I suppose I can't really make these sorts of assumptions as it will add to the young Asian stereotype and we hate stereotypes. At first stereotypes are funny but as soon as someone gets offended that's it, the walls come tumbling down and everyone gets offended and if you don't! Then you are the problem.

My next stop is about a ten minute walk away but because I'm masked up and it's warm let's make it a twenty minute walk and enjoy the moment. Enjoy being a murderous old Asian man for a while.

After a few minutes of walking I think I'll make this a thirty minute walk. It's warmer than I thought, and I don't like it.

On my way I walk past a chicken place. Andover seems like such a long time ago now. I'm tempted to pop in and grab a quick bite to eat, but with an online rating of just 2.0 out of 5, I think I'll give it a miss. It's strange though. The place has a terrible rating, yet from where I'm standing it looks busy enough. Just goes to show, customer opinion is totally pointless. If someone wants to eat shit food, they will seek out and enjoy shit food regardless of how amazing you believe your opinion to be.

I eventually shuffle my way to Commercial Street and its a lot busier than I had anticipated so I take a tiny diversion down Gomond Street and take refuge in one of the empty shop doorways. I take my hoodie out of my bag, lay it upon the ground and wait. I know what I'm doing, it's all under control.
I sat waiting for almost 3 hours and finally the moment arrived I had been waiting for. A shifty looking skinny bloke with bad teeth and stained clothing stands above me. He looks rough yet his Nike Air Max trainers look brand new.

Ey mush, wanna buy some weed.

Eh!

Wanna buy some weed, spice or I can get you some skag mate if you want it.

Come closer I can't hear you.

At this point I no longer have my protective surgical mask on, but to be honest I have just put on quite possibly the most offensive accent I have ever done. Apologies to any Chinese people reading this, it wasn't intentional.

Mate, I can get you whatever you need.

Come sit, let's talk. I have money.

Oh yeh money. Sweet.

The moment this scummy Northerner sits down I thrust my knife deep into his neck. This is becoming a favourite place of mine now. Not slicing or cutting but diving the blade straight into the throat and with the serrated edge pushing downwards, allowing my victims life to escape through the wound.
As he falls, I push him into the ground and cover the blood best I can with my hoodie. The fucker is still moving so I am obliged to penetrate him yet again.
I'm not sure where his head is so I just keep punching him with my blade in the area I think would end his life

the quickest, and a few thrusts later, he is no longer moving. I pause for breath and its then that I can see his blood slowly making its way out from under my hoodie, into the shop doorway and onto the pedestrian walkway. I need to move, and fast.

I manage a few feet before panic takes control. I dive into another of the empty shop doorways. This has gone wrong. Why the fuck am I Chinese? I hate this situation, sometimes. Now it begins, the fucking internal battle with myself. The silent voice against the silent voice. Everything happening inside my head and even though it's mine, I'm not in control. Who is? Who is having these conversations? All I'm doing is physically battling against it, punching the air and screaming at nothing. Having three way, four way conversations in my own brain and I have to fight to regain control.

The body has been found and a lot quicker than I had expected. I curl up in the doorway and pretend I'm dead. You know, like when you're a kid and you pretend to be dead. Basically, just lying on the floor and, well that's it really, but as a kid it's super realistic! With that in mind this should work just as well, being motionless and Chinese or Asian, or whatever I'm pretending to be.

No, I can't be Chinese right now. The police will no doubt want to move me on or question me and they will see through this disguise straight away, so mask off and suddenly become a homeless white dude. Fuck!

I wait with closed eyes but open ears, trying to digest every sound I can.
As I lay there as still as a rock, I remember one of my earliest pets, he was a rock. Well, more of a stone really. He was kept in a cage and had googly eyes. I'm sure he had name, but I'm fucked if I can remember what it was. Rocky or something like that would be a good guess.

Excuse me sir. Sir, hello excuse me.

For a moment there I thought I was back on the train. Isn't this exactly what the guard said?

There has been an incident can you please stand up. We may need to ask you some questions.

I stand up, get my belongings as suggested and begin to vacate the area. The officer shouts back at me saying I need to return to the scene as a potential witness, but he can't control everything. The curious crowd is getting larger and the second officer is busy dealing with the person who found the body so try as he might, he's not going to convince me to return to this shit show.

My thirty-minute walk into Hereford is now an eight minute stomp.
Once on the train my next stop is Birmingham, then onto Derby where I need to spend some time both on my own and with Ana. I've really missed her.

TWELVE : AVIANA

I woke up happy this morning because I woke up next to Aviana, or Ana as she prefers to be called. She is here in my bed and she is a prostitute, my prostitute. I pay her £2000 a month and have done so for the past eight months. What I pay her for is to be here when I need her. Not just to be my fuck toy, but to hold me and remind me that humans are allowed to be happy. The problem is, I spent years telling myself I couldn't be happy and that I didn't deserve to be happy. If I was then I would be punished. Nothing good ever happens, so why start trying? I was told time and time again to set the bar low in life so you will never be disappointed, and you never have to try. That way, you will never fail. If that's the case, then what is the point in being alive? I am allowed to be happy. I keep telling myself that I am allowed to be happy. If happiness wasn't normal, then why do babies laugh?

Right now, I am happy. Ana walks out of the shower and switches on the TV. She looks amazing naked. Twenty five years old, five foot tall with long dark hair and the most beautiful breasts. Her skin is amazing. It is covered in hundreds of tiny hands, so no matter what part of her I'm touching, she is holding me. Not a skinny girl, she is all natural. Curvy and pervy. I look at every inch of *Dani* and she is so perfect. The way she lines her toes up is so clever. Always in order and always so smooth.

Sometimes, when she's been on her feet all day, she lets me curl up at the foot of the bed, chair or wherever and just be near her feet. They are so warm, and the clammy smell doesn't put me off. In fact, I quite like it. Pushing my nose in-between her toes and just enjoying the moment. It's nothing sexual, I just enjoy it. Sometimes me and the toes dance together. I hum a strange, staggered little tune and just like a snake charmer sat in an old dusty street with a cobra in a basket, the toes dance and sway in time to the music. Except I haven't defanged them or sewn their mouths shut.
Ana looks over at me and interrupts my thinking.

You ok.

Hmmm?

You ok? You're just staring at me with a silly grin on your face.

Yeah, I'm just feeling content right now. Happy.

Silly man. I'll put the kettle on. Cup of tea?

I could kill her so easily. Knife the life out of her or strangle her in her sleep. Suffocate her with a pillow or make it look like a suicide. Drug her, drag her into the bath, slit her wrists and leave her there. With a suicide note of course, but I can't. She means too much to me at the moment, plus she is really good at her job. She is my sexy, fleshy security blanket. Ok, I'll be honest that sounds gross, but you get where I'm coming from.

An hour has passed since she left and I'm still in bed. I've never had any real success with girls growing up. I had a girlfriend when I was 5 and then nothing until I was 16. After that business picked up, but I was a terrible shag. If I had the confidence back then that I have now I would have been a prolific lover. I never had a problem getting girls to like me. I looked good with my long hair and my make it up as I go along sense of style, plus I was living away from home so that was considered cool, yet I never had a proper sexual relationship until I was 19. Up until that point I was just happy to know someone fancied me and once we'd kissed, I wanted to move on. I would go to college parties and if I hadn't pulled within an hour, I would target the lower rung of the ladder and pick a girl from there. They were always up for it and numerous times would try and take me to bed but I would refuse. Not because I was a gentleman, but because I just didn't want to get to that point. I had confidence in spades when it came to flirting and making someone feel special, but it was just that final act I couldn't commit to. For me it was the final barrier to exposing the real me, and that is something no one was allowed to access.

I look back and think of all the missed opportunities. I remember one girl in particular, her name was Sam. We would have both been around 17/18 years old and she was naturally beautiful. Not attractive, beautiful. Slim with red hair and white, flawless skin. We really liked each other and the first time we got the chance to be alone I knew we were going to have sex.

We kissed for what seemed like hours and when she undressed in front of me, I could not believe my luck. This was going to be amazing. I took off my clothes and we moved onto the floor. I kissed every part of her and without words she told me she was ready. We were about to make love. This wasn't just a fuck, this was building up to be more than that. I was going to make love to the most beautiful girl I had ever met, and it was at this point that I did something that I would regret forever. I faked an asthma attack. Why? Panic. Nerves. I have no idea, but something within me decided that a fake asthma attack was the best way to get out of this. But get out of what! I wanted this to happen and so did she. Who decided it was time for me to bail out with the most pathetic of excuses? Safe to say that Sam was not impressed, and we never really spoke after that. Sadly, this wasn't the only time I used this awful excuse to get out of having sex with someone. It happened at least 3 more times with 3 different girls from what I can remember, and once I achieved sexual liberation with someone, I could never stay faithful. Ever.

Today, I no longer care. I don't pursue women in the way I used to. Even if I do attract someone when I'm out and about it's not long before I return to form and fail at the final hurdle. If I want sex, I pay. This way it's on my terms, when I want it and if it's a massive fail then it doesn't matter. Your opinion doesn't matter and neither does your life.

I pay, you perform, I cum, you leave and within a few minutes I've forgotten about whoever you are, except for Ana. She is the exception.

THIRTEEN : IPSWICH

I met John Taylor in 2012 at a book signing in Bristol. John Taylor being the bass player from Duran Duran and for a number of years my absolute idol. I would spend hours upon hours of my teenage years learning his bass lines, and this was way before Guitar Tab type websites appeared. I used to buy piano/keyboard music books, learn the chords, figure out the reason for those notes within the structure of said chord, be it a minor, major, diminished or augmented, and from that I would dissect each and every song until I worked out the bass line and why he chose those specific notes. I mastered the whole of the first album and a select number of my favourite tracks from the music that followed. In time my taste in music moved to rock with bands like Bon Jovi, Guns N' Roses and from there the rock got heavier as I was introduced to bands such as Fear Factory, Carcass and Pantera, to name a few. Over the years my tastes moved beyond English-speaking bands as I discovered a new wave of music from the Far East, Japan in particular. The music is as brutal as it is peaceful. The vocals range from sweet Japanese whispered tones to a full guttural growl. I love the blended mix of silk and sandpaper together in the same song. Highlights just how repetitive and unoriginal mainstream music has now become. Musicians are products, not artists. Manufactured before our very eyes and sold to the lowest bidder.

RAMBLE ALERT!!
Enough of that. Back to this particular evening in Bristol.

I remember arriving late, as in I was way down the line to get in, so I knew my only option was to turn on the charm and get as far to the front as I could. I got chatting to a group of people who were talking about their favourite DD track. I butted in with 'Secret Oktober'—which was the B-side to Union of the Snake. If you don't know what a B-side is then you've missed out on one of the music industries greatest treats. Like the 12" single. An extended version of the original song and two B-sides.
Secret Oktober was the answer I gave and one that could only be delivered by a true Durannie. With this I was accepted into their group. Throw on top my little story about having to travel over seventy miles to be at this event, and suddenly I had everyone on my side. Once we entered the venue, I purchased my book and followed my new best friends to the main auditorium where JT was going to be appearing on stage and entertaining us for the evening.
I secured a seat at the front and near some stairs which led up to the stage where I guessed the book signings would happen at the end. At least I hoped so.

Seeing John Taylor walk out on stage was amazing. I sat happily through the memories that my hero was sharing with us, and at the end it was time for the book signings and yes, I got to the front of the queue which was amazing, not only because I got to speak to JT before he got bored of saying the same old answers to the same old questions, but also it gave me time to leave the venue and run, literally run to the train station to get the last train home.

As JT signed my book, someone in his team asked if I wanted a photo taken with him to which I declined as I needed to get out and get my train home. Instead, I shook his beautiful hand, thanked him for the memories and ran out of the venue. I still have the book and his signature is in perfect condition within. If I'm honest with you, I'm never going to read it for fear of ruining it. It's perfect as it is.

Why am I telling you this? Because today everything kind of went wrong. I'm in Ipswich and I am sleeping out on the street, but it's not that bad.

So, why didn't I stay and have my photo taken with JT and just sleep rough for the night? It's something I've done countless times since, and I'm doing it again tonight. Why didn't I just stay? I don't know, but I didn't, and that's that.
As I was saying, Ipswich today did not go smoothly. Maybe it was because I got complacent and just thought I'd repeat what I did all that time ago in Basingstoke, except this time I didn't book a hotel. I just arrived at the station, got changed and popped on my middle-

aged man mask, with specs and all the other bits, and headed straight to the NCP on Foundation Street. I made my way to the second floor and waited for someone to return to their car so I could do the confused, can't remember where I parked routine. Within 10 minutes I saw a lady walking out onto the car park floor and toward her car.

Can I help you?

I'm somewhat confused. I can't remember where I parked.

You sure. There are only like, five cars up here.

Sorry my love I can't hear you.

I shuffle a little closer to her ready to launch my attack. She is shorter than me, slim build wearing light blue jeans and a white polo shirt. I can't really make out the face as she has accessorised her head with a baseball cap and sunglasses. Either way, she doesn't look like she'll be too difficult to dispose of.

Are you wearing a mask?

I beg your pardon. What do you mean?

I've worked enough TV shows to know. I can see you're wearing a mask.

Sorry love you'll have to come closer.

In another life I feel I would know this woman. So much so that it's making me panic and when I panic, I start to sweat. Not the best thing to do whilst trying to maintain composure and kill someone.

As she walks toward me, a drop of sweat falls into my eye causing me to drop my guard for the briefest of moments but that is all she needs.
With a swift kick she knocks me off balance. The next kick is the one that knocks me off my feet. As I attempt to stand up, she hits me again. What the fuck is this! What is going on? She grabs my mask and pulls it off my face. I immediately hide myself behind my hands and run off toward the exit, like the coward I didn't know I was.

You better run you little freak!

I did just that. Before I knew it, I have ended up on Turret Lane and I have no idea where that is in relation to the few locations I've memorised for this journey. There's an open gate to the back of some building which looks like a good place to stop and take stock of what just happened.

I got my ass kicked, that's what just happened. The bitch said she worked TV shows but what is she, a stuntwoman, a fucking kicking expert? Worst of all, she has my mask. I don't care about what it cost me; I care that she may keep it. I care that this could be one major fuck up and be the exposure I can do without. I hope she has just binned it and forgotten about it.
Hopefully, I'm just another freak who has got his ass whooped by her and she can go home knowing the streets are safe for one more night.
Why didn't I just run behind her and slice open her fucking neck? Stab her in the head and piss all over her dying body. FUCK!

I've been sat here for an hour and calmed down enough that I can work out what to do next. I need to make my way back to the station, but I still have to complete the letter I. My paranoia is through the roof right now and I'm feeling sick, but I can't pull out now, or can I? This is my game and I decide the rules. No, I don't. Who am I kidding? The game has already been created, and they set the rules. I'm the player, not the creator.
I get my stuff together and start walking. I don't want to use my phone because I need the battery to last as I think I'm going to be here for the night. I'm only on 21% and that's not good.

Walking out of Turret Lane, I spot a church. I cross over the road and head round to the front of the building. The gates are locked but that's ok, the wall is low enough to climb over. Once inside the grounds I realise just how small this plot of land is. There isn't much shelter, but I guess I could kip here if I need to.

Excuse me, you shouldn't be in there.

I turn, and there's a white-haired old woman standing on the other side of the wall.

I say, you shouldn't be in there when it's closed.

Fuck off!

That shut her up, and she did exactly what she is told and fucks off. I'm not in the mood to be polite, fake or otherwise. Hang on, hang on! She would have been a perfect hit. I could have walked over to her, be all apologetic, and once she let her guard down, drag her over the wall and finish her. No threat of getting my arse kicked there. But I didn't. I really need to focus. What is wrong with me today?

I lay my jacket on the ground and sit. If I could cry, I would. If I could allow myself to be human for a moment, I would cry. The emptiness I feel right now is numbing and the numbing sensation adds to the sense of vulnerability, but it is short-lived as that other me creeps back in and takes over.

If our eyes acted like mood rings, that would be pretty amazing. You could watch as someone went from red to black to blue to green. Do the rings work though, or were they just a quick cash in when everyone was all about relaxing to whale song and shit like that? Do those colours mean anything anyway, or is it all down to how hot you are? Body temperature would make it change colour, wouldn't it?

I'm sure there are plenty of fluffy, spiritual people out there who could bore the living shit out of me with stories about what all the colours signify and how they pass over into your day-to-day life, but it's all bullshit. Just because you say it softly doesn't mean it's true. I've been told through my various therapy sessions that I should try meditation, mindfulness and grounding techniques but none of them work, not for me anyway. Dream Catchers, remember them! Feathers and some fabric in a hoop used in Native American cultures before common sense and knowledge was invented. Same applies here with the church. The house of God. Problem is, God was never here. This is just a building designed to house fear and control. Much like our modern day media, fear and control. Creating division and spewing hatred, but in the most subtle of ways and those of us unaware, fall for it every time.

It's dark now, and I'm cold. All I have is my jacket and a change of clothes. I tried putting my clothes on top of the clothes I'm wearing now but that ended up being so uncomfortable so instead I'm trying to fashion some

kind of bedding out of a pair of jeans, a t-shirt and a hoodie. It's really not working but I'm tired so I'm sure I'll fall asleep at some point. As I stare up at the empty sky, I remember the stories my father used to share with me about the stars. How far away they were. How many light years it would take to get there. How big the universe is. These conversations were always best when we sat in the New Forest with a couple of cold cans and a sparkly blanket of possibilities above our heads.
The conversation would always follow the same pattern and end with a remark about how insignificant it must make you feel to exist in a universe as vast as this. Those moments, were very few and far between but they were special. I need to go back and repeat this one day, but as for the question around feeling insignificant. No, I do not feel insignificant. I did once, but not anymore.

I check my phone, it's 3.49am. I think I've managed a few hours sleep which is more than I was expecting, so can't complain. I'm going to move on and head toward the station. My phone has 13% battery, enough to get maps up and work out where I am.

It appears I'm about fifteen minutes away from the station so not too bad, I'll take a slow walk as I don't want to get there too early.

The roads are quiet as the people of Ipswich are still asleep. The streets deserted. Halfway through my journey, I pass an empty car park. Empty except for, I think I can make out a tent pitched up in the far corner. This has to be it. This has to be the one so I can get out of here and back to Derby. I pause for a moment and rummage through my bag to see what I have available. Perfect. Blades and a lighter. Sounds like a country and western song; Blades and a Lighter, blah, blah, American banjos, blah, blah, I fucked my sister, blah, blah, Yankee doodle day.

I slowly make my way over to the tent. It's so dark and I can't use my phone as a light as the battery is pretty much empty. There are no streetlights in this car park, but the moon sheds a little light on the area, plus my eyes have adjusted to the darkness through which I have walked. I make it to the tent and hope there is someone inside. I'm tempted to peek in and check, but I dare not.

What if there are children inside? What if it's empty? What if the tent owner is stood behind you right now?

STOP! Leave me the fuck alone.

I set fire to the bottom corner of the tent and within a few seconds those questions have been answered as the zip at the front opens.

Before the man could even stand, I plunged my knife into the back of his neck and then kicked him as hard as

I could. He fell to the floor but staggered up onto his hands and knees. I stabbed again, and again, and again. I had to stop as by this point his tent was fully engulfed in flames. I put the knife back in my bag and dragged the guy as near to his tent as I could so his body would catch fire. I also threw the clothes I no longer needed into the burning tent. It was then I had a thought. I grabbed my phone, 9% battery, and took a photo. Put the phone back in my pocket and made my escape. Thanks to the orange glow of the burning man, I could now see where I was going and could leave the car park a lot quicker than I entered it.

Once outside I wasn't really sure where to go, but I was able to find a moment of solitude behind the bins next to the closed retail outlets and made sure I just stayed put for a couple of hours.

6. 6. 6.

I breathe and calm myself down. The sun is rising, and birds are starting their morning chorus. Sirens fly past as the news of a burning tent has reached the appropriate people. A few minutes later an ambulance goes past. I wait. Wait until my mind and body are totally calm then I will know it is time to continue to the station. I check my phone, it's 7.14am. I get to my feet and head to the station and back to Derby, where I intend to sleep for about 3 days.
Ipswich, I hope we never meet again.

FOURTEEN : JARROW

Mary said to me. Boy, you'd better believe, that if you died, you would not be alive to appreciate the fact you're dead.

Self-destruction, self-harm and suicidal thoughts have been a part of my life for so long now that I can't remember not feeling that way. Although I do not believe in any kind of afterlife I did once have an out-of-body experience, I think. I was in my late teens or early twenties, living in a shared house with a couple of friends and working at an animal rescue. Sounds idyllic doesn't it, and it kind of was.
House parties, garden sex, and extreme home makeovers. What I mean by that is one night we found some dirt on the kitchen ceiling and tried to remove it with a broom, but it kind of went wrong and the ceiling fell down. It looked ok, so we left it.

On the night of my out-of-body experience, I remember dreaming that someone had shot me in the stomach. The moment this happened, I recall drifting above my bed. Feeling light yet somehow weighted. I carried on floating and looking down I could see myself on the bed, peaceful. There was no noise or stress, but that was broken the moment I woke up. Not only did I remember the entire event, but I also had an incredible pain in my stomach where I had been shot. There was no visible or physical injury to show to anyone, just the pain of where the bullet penetrated my skin. For a moment I was terrified. Did I really leave my body? No, I couldn't have because that makes no sense. Logically, it doesn't add up.

For this to happen you must have a soul, a spirit.

Not this again.

For this to happen you must have a soul, a spirit.

I know and I'm saying I don't have a soul. Pigs, flamingos and cockroaches don't have a soul or a higher purpose, so why should I?

How can you float above and see yourself if you didn't leave your body.

It's a memory of a dream and for years it has stuck with me as something I could never really explain.

What you're saying is that after all that it was just a dream.

Yes.

What about the pain you felt?

I don't know, I can't answer that. Maybe I just had stomach pain and, in my dream, it warped into someone shooting me.

Did you see a light as you drifted above your empty body.

No there wasn't a light.

Did you see Jesus.

No, I didn't see Jesus.

Did any of this actually happen?

Yes! You were there. Maybe it was you I was trying to leave.

What does that mean?

Maybe I need to be separated from you.

Go on then do it, kill yourself. That's the only way you can ever get away from me.

I will, but when I decide to, and when I do, I do not want to die alone or in my sleep. I need to know that when I'm dead, I'm dead. If I died peacefully in my sleep, I would feel it cheated me out of my last moments. When my eyes close for the final time I want it to be on

my terms. I want to end my time on this rock the right way. There is still so much I have yet to master.
I can't move objects with my mind yet when I'm asleep I can. I can't fly or fight yet in my dreams I can.
I've always been a mouthy little asshole but never been much of a fighter, especially in a one-on-one confrontation. I prefer the odds to be stacked against me. A minimum of 3 people to fight with.
Again, not because I'm super tough, but because I can take a punch. I can take a beating and it freaks people out when you absorb the pain and then stand up ready for more. Someone once said to me I scared them, not physically but mentally. I had a look about me that suggested I was unpredictable and dangerous.
My family thought for a long time that I was schizo, this was back in the day when schizophrenic / schizo was just a phrase used to describe a mentally unstable person.

Language was easier back then. No one got offended because everyone was honest, and you knew your place. If I listed some common phrases used by my grandparents to describe the owners of the corner shop, or my black friend who lived a few doors down from them, that would cause great offense. What about the names the Indian kids who lived on my street called me? I reckon that one is ok because that wouldn't be racist.

Spastic, I can probably say that because we're not scared of upsetting the disabled. We can also mock the Christian belief in God because there is no threat from Christians. Other religious groups are not so lenient, so we avoid mocking them.
Hypocrisy and double standards, the cornerstone of the Western World.

SUICIDE

We read that someone has died by suicide and we instantly shout out from behind our screens that this person should have reached out. Should have just opened up and talked. Yeah, because that's the solution isn't it.
How about we fill in the cracks of society with all your generic slogans and maybe then, those who had taken their own lives would never have got to that point.

He was a great man.
She was an incredible woman. So caring and talented.
We were always there for him.
We never thought for a moment she would choose to end her own life.

It's easy to mourn a victim of suicide. You can say all the lines you've heard others say. You can indulge in the act of mourning and self-pity because you tried so hard to save them, but you couldn't. You can use the event to remove this feeling of self-imposed guilt and believe that just because you couldn't save his life, you can still save others. Well, I hate to break it to you, but you can't.

I'm in Jarrow and currently stood on a footbridge above the metro track. I am not wearing a mask or any kind of covering today, because today I don't fucking care. I don't care if I'm caught. I don't care if my killing spree ends at the letter J. I am happy for this to all be over now.

Only kidding.
Can you imagine if I did that? Just suddenly stopped and destroyed all the work I have done so far just because I had a surge of guilt? Folkestone was a glitch and that feeling of guilt will never resurface. Today, I will be aiding someone in their own suicide. I've always wanted to kill someone this way. I used to walk home over a bridge that, at its highest point has a 90-foot drop. My favourite time to venture onto the bridge was between 11pm and 1am, as there would always be a couple of drunks walking home this way. I imagined that I would follow slowly behind one of these individuals, and when we reach the middle of the bridge, I would attack and force them over the side and into the black water below.
No one would be witness to the attack and no one would know they were in the water until someone had

either submitted a missing person claim or the body washed up somewhere. Either way, it looks like a drunken suicide or tomfoolery gone wrong. No way of tracing it back to me and I can continue to go about my daily business as normal.

I have yet to put this plan into action, but today I will. I've been lurking around the area for several hours now. I arrived here from York, got myself changed and have been pretending to be a train enthusiast for the past couple of hours and Oh Lordy! It's a tedious existence, but one that has delivered a fantastic yield.
I got chatting to a group of these choochoo chasers and struck up quite a good rapport with one of them who goes by the name, Dorset (That's what he calls himself, his real name is Kenny Westerly but thinks Dorset makes him sound cool—his words, not mine) and he said he'd meet me back here an hour later.
Once I knew he had gone, I headed off to a secluded area and got into my change of clothes and new mask. I had this delivered just a few weeks back, and it is so cute. It's quite different to what I've worn before, mainly because it cost me over £2,000 but it is so worth it. It has a full head of hair, realistic eyebrows and a short beard. It's really comfortable to wear as well. It's going to look so good on CCTV. Kind of wishing it got delivered sooner, but I will certainly get at least one more use out of this.

I'm now back at the station waiting for my new best friend. As his train pulls into the station, I take my phone out of my pocket and lift it to my face. Dorset walks past me, all smiles as he looks out for his new friend. Me.

It looks like he's been home and got changed because I'm sure he had jeans and a green jumper on earlier. Now he's turned up in dark trousers and a well pressed, checked shirt. As he walks up onto the footbridge, I wonder what he thinks this meeting is? Maybe he's going on somewhere else after? Shame because he will not make it.
I look at him one last time, take a deep breath and make my move. It's quiet, so it's now or never.
I lift my phone to my ear and pretend to have a conversation. I end up arguing with my imaginary caller as they have told me to wait on the wrong platform. I put the phone down and advance toward the footbridge.

As I walk up the final few steps, I can see Dorset smiling at me. He makes some joke about being on the wrong platform, to which I hysterically agree. When he turns his back to me that is when I attack. I grab the back of his head and ram it against the concrete wall. I pull his head back and yank down his bottom jaw, ramming him once again into the wall. He collapses to the floor, making some weird noises and bellowing WHY repeatedly. At this point I drive my knee as hard as I can

into his face, making his head collide once again with that same wall. Now he is quiet.
I check the time and it looks like the train is due in 3 minutes. I pull a piece of paper out of my pocket and place it into the trouser pocket of this pointless fag. As he lay crumpled at my feet, I almost feel sorry for him, but that sensation soon passes. It's his fault he's here, not mine.

The station is slowly starting to get a little busier but not enough for me to worry, yet. I slide my knife into my jacket sleeve just in case someone ventures up the stairs. I don't really want to make this a multiple murder, but I will if I have to.

The train is due is 90 seconds. I bend down and lift the limp body of this prick onto my shoulders. He is still alive as I can feel his heart beating against the back of my neck. I face away from the station and dump Dorset off the footbridge and onto the tracks below. As soon as I hear his body hit the ground, I turn away and walk to the opposite platform.
Within seconds the silence is broken as the air is shattered by a violent scream.

There is a body on the tracks!

The usual, predictable mix of panic, fear and confusion grips the few people on the platform. I sit down on an empty bench and observe.

One person is on the phone, another is running toward the body on the tracks in the hope they can provide some kind of rescue and Dorset himself is starting to move.

This is concerning me.

He lifts one arm and tries to move his body so he can stand up. Nearby people are trying to reach out to him. With whatever strength he has left he manages to get to his knees but it's too late. The train arrives and ends his life. It doesn't hit him with great speed but does so with enough force that he is dragged under and there is no way he is walking away from that. It all appeared to happen in slow motion. I wonder if he felt it all in slow motion? The metal face of the train smacking into his back and shattering his spine and ribs as it forces its way through him. The sheer weight dragging him forward and smashing his distorted face into the gravel below. His skin being peeled off as easily as a hungry ape would peel the skin from a banana, and I'm not sure what part of him made the cracking noise, but it was satisfying.

The people on the platform are horrified. I'm relieved. The train comes to a grinding halt as the driver jumps out shouting that he didn't see him and that he is sorry. Someone has walked up onto the footbridge and is looking down at the track on which my victim fell. He looks over at me. It is then I realise that I am the only person not projecting a sense of panic or fear. I am the only person still sat on a bench.

We stare at each other for a few seconds and it is at this point I stand up and walk away. My next stop is Hebburn which I will travel to on foot. It's less than a couple of miles away but this will give me time to not only change out of this disguise but to also vanish from the eyes of any CCTV that might be monitoring my journey. From Hebburn I'll head to Newcastle then back down to York.

Compared to the mess that was Ipswich, this went surprisingly well. Just a few more places to tick off the list and I'll be halfway there.

FIFTEEN : KIDDERMINSTER

Imagine standing in an empty room and everything is black. Not painted black but everything is dark, so totally dark, void of light and alone you stand. You do not know if you are in the middle of the room, near the wall or even how big the room is. Reaching out, you feel nothing.

Before moving, you need to work out if you were even facing the right way to begin with? Without direction or light, how do you know?
Which way should you turn? Should you run or walk? Crawling is not an option as no man should be on his knees unless he is asking for forgiveness. Do you think you need to ask for forgiveness? Do you think you've done something wrong? Of course not, so the choice is to run or walk, but why do you have to move at all?

You want to move because you need to escape the dark. You want to move because you haven't been told to stand still. You want to move because you are scared.

The words and whispers that kept you calm are becoming louder and more intrusive. They scream and demand that you listen to every instruction and act without question. Muddled and confused, you try and understand what they are asking but the voices are so loud, intense. There is no space to think! There is no space to be alone. In a room so dark, so black and empty, it feels so crowded. Yet, the room is silent. The shadows that stood by you remain invisible, confirming that they were nothing more than a trick of the mind, yet you know you are not alone.

The room is empty, black and never ending, and you need to escape. You need to get out. In front of you is a door, and scribbled across the door frame in black ink are the words; *the only way out of the darkness would be to work out how you got there in the first place*. But it's not as simple as, simply opening the door.

The door presents to you three options;

1. Walking through the door could be life changing and get you the answers and closure you need to regain control of your life.
2. You open the door and after a long walk you just end up back in the room, but his time it's louder, more intrusive and the only door available to you is one that leads you suicide. If you survive, the room gets painted white.
3. You turn your back on the door and walk back into the darkness and accept that this is your life. Never getting better but never getting worse. Existing, not living. Emotionally dead, yet alive.

I chose to walk through that door when I went into therapy. My thought process was to go and find a way out of the darkness. Problem was, the fool I was talking to couldn't find the light switch. I doubt she could even use a torch or know which end to light the candle. Just delivering tiresome question after tiresome question, grinding me down and achieving nothing but personal regret for agreeing to take these sessions in the first place. An absolute waste of time and funding. It's safe to say that I ended up back in the black room. It's still dark, overcrowded and empty. I don't like it and I don't want to stay here anymore but I know the only way out of this, is to walk back through that door and accept my fate. But I don't believe in fate, destiny or luck. Nothing is planned out for us and there is no greater, divine plan. We have no soul or spirituality, if you think differently then that's your problem.

Everything is decided by the decisions we make. Nothing is left to chance and I'll do my best to explain why. Instead of using names I'm just going to use letters. A- Alice, B- Ben and so on. Right, here goes and remember, this is just an example.

A and **B** have an argument which results in **A** leaving for work in an angry mood.
Whilst driving, **A** doesn't look where she's going and crashes into a car driven by **C**.
B calls into work and fakes a sick day so he can be alone. This means **E** will have to work longer hours to cover his absence.
E calls her partner **F**, but she is not answering. **E** leaves a voicemail letting her know she'll be late home.

A is at the hospital with minor injuries but is ok.
A decides enough is enough and will leave **B** as she has been seeing **S** for the past 4 months and no longer has feelings for **B**.
F listens to her voicemail and cancels her evening plans to go and pick up **E** from work when she finishes her shift.
C has his car towed away and takes the rest of the day off work. He is his own boss so it's not a big deal. He walks into a newsagent on the way home and purchases 2 lottery scratch cards. He wins £2 on the first one and £200 on the second one.
Soon after **G** makes the same purchase from the same shop and wins nothing.
G bumps into **H** who wants to be paid, but **G** has no money.
E is about to walk out of the building when she hears a scream. Rushing outside she sees that **F** has been attacked. She is ok but is the victim of a mugging. Her phone and bag have been stolen.
E drives them both home.
H accepts the stolen items as payment from **G.**
F calls in to work and explains what happened last night and takes the day off with **E** who suggests they leave the city and move back to the countryside where they both met.
This could go on for (p)ages but I'll leave it there. By using this tiny example though you can see what I'm saying. If **A** hadn't crashed into **C**, then **F** would never have been mugged.

If I walked out of the door stepped on a mouse and killed it, was that my fault? I didn't disturb the mouse. I didn't force it to run across my path.
When I ended the life of that woman in Cambridge, it wasn't my fault. Someone else made me into who I am today. Someone else is to blame.

SEE SAW

What's your favourite horror film?

I guess a more difficult question would be, why?
Why that particular film. For me it's the SAW series of films. Why? Because they were gory and creative. I like that.

Growing up I liked the Puppet Master films and I also watched a lot of Asian horror and gore. The films Sick Nurses, Doll Master, Ichi the Killer and Battle Royale come to mind. Don't forget those Asian classics which have been destroyed by American remakes, such as Oldboy and The Grudge.

I don't know if this applies to your particular film choice but I know you've seen it done, and that is when the bad guy hides on the back seats of someone's car and then suddenly pops up ready to indulge in some kind of dastardly shenanigans, well that's what I want to do and I found the perfect place. Big supermarket car park. Loads of potential victims and plenty of parking spaces. I'm going in unmasked as well as I feel the good people of Kidderminster deserve to see my beautiful face.

My location is a nice fifteen-minute stroll from the station and the location in question is the car park adjacent to the large supermarket and yes, I am going to recreate that very scene and if I get caught, I'm going to blame it all on video violence.

Have you noticed how excessively violent 12 and 15 certificate films are. When I was a kid a film with a 15 certificate was usually one with a lot of swearing or excessive violence.
Any sign of bloodshed was more often than not saved for those labelled with an 18 certificate.
Comic book movies are the same, but because it's portrayed as fantasy violence, it's ok to be released with a 12 or 12a certificate. And of course, with that comes the obligatory wave of merchandise which is produced and aimed at a much lower age group.
Should we be promoting violence to children?

Saying that, buy a three year old some dinosaurs and the first thing it is most likely going to do is make a roaring noise followed by the inevitable dino showdown as these plastic behemoths go head to head in a fight to the death. Which makes me consider the idea that we are born with an understanding of violence, and as porn and violence become more and more accessible, maybe we are just becoming immune to its effects. Maybe death and sex are no longer taboo subjects. If that's the case, then what is?

By this point I am stood in the car park, at the back end near the trolley shed, thing. I don't know what these are called so today it's called the trolley shed. I don't even have time to get my phone out of my pocket to pretend to make a phone call when I spot my target.

He's an older chap, I'd say somewhere between the age of 55 – 85? I have no idea. I just see what I need to see. An old guy popping his shopping into the back of his car, with a trolley that he will need to return which will give me the time I need to get into his car and do what I was born to do, administer violence upon him. Administer, Kidderminster. Does that rhyme? No, not really. Spinster works, but I don't know what a spinster is. The Kidderminster Spinster. Now that's a superhero name you could build a franchise on.

Like the idea I had the other day about a junior highwayman and his liver who is also his best friend and sidekick. It's called **Stan and his Liver**.

The old guy is walking toward the trolley shed now so it's my time to move. His left his front door open so this is not going to be a problem.

I open the door, unlock the back door and sneak onto the seat behind the driver. FYI, I have gloves on and under my gloves I've created some kind of glove sheath out of plastic bags. My hands are super sweaty, but I have the grip still from the gloves and my thinking is that the moisture and extra protection will disguise my fingerprints enough.
The back seat is disgusting as this guy clearly has a dog(s). There are a couple of shopping bags back here as well. I have a quick glance inside. Lemons, milk, prune juice, cheese and old people biscuits.
I can hear him coming toward the car and he's talking to someone. As they say their goodbyes, he opens the car door. He then closes the car door, but the problem is he is still on the outside of the car. The door locks. What the fuck. Where is he going? This isn't how it plays out in the movies.

Imagine this, I am laying on the floor of an old guys car wearing carrier bag gloves trying to think up creative recipes for lemons, milk, prune juice, cheese and old people biscuits whilst trying not to sneeze because of all the fucking dog hair.

He has been gone so long. I hope he hasn't died. How the fuck would I explain this if he died in the supermarket and the Police opened the doors to the car and found me here. Five more minutes pass and he is still not back. My left arm has gone numb because of the position I've been in for the past 10 minutes and I'm starting to get really pissed off, but I can hear footsteps outside the car, and here he is. Finally, but I can't move because my bastard arm has gone to sleep. He starts the car and puts on the radio which is a blessing as I can now rearrange myself into a more comfortable position ready to attack, but I've had an idea. I notice he didn't put his seatbelt on which I guess means we're not going to be in the car for that long, but hopefully I'll have long enough to get this done.

As we slowly make our way out of the car park I look up at the old guy and imagine what he has done for the past 60 or 70 years. I'm sure he's a grandad and most probably a great grandad. Maybe even a great, great grandad. What does that even mean? Having someone that shares the tiniest thread of your bloodline being forced upon you every now and then. As you decay physically and mentally, this child is presented to you as something for you to be proud of. Why? Its young, happy, innocent face is full of wonder and excitement. Yours is old, loose and grey.

Full of liver spots and creases. You have nothing in common with this creature, yet you provide it with hugs and material goods that will be forgotten about, as will you. You will become nothing but a photograph and a story.
As I look at this old man, I wonder what he thinks about. Inside that old grey head of his, does he have any ambition left or is it just a case of eat, sleep, repeat until

the repeat finally comes to an end?
He is now singing along to something, Cliff Richard I think? The Young Ones? Ironic title really considering he no longer fits into that category. He looks happy enough singing along to it, or at least to most of the words anyway.

I wait until we are moving at speed and take a sneaky glance out of the window. We are on a wide stretch of road and I think we've just come off a roundabout. I pull the milk out of the bag, remove the lid and start pouring. The old guy soon notices the milk spilling onto his floor as the bottle drains between the two front seats and this is my moment. As he is looking down to his left, I plunged my blade into his head. Just behind the right ear.
The car spins wildly out of control, we hit something and roll. This is terrifying and again, I don't believe this is how it happens in the movies. Fuck! I cling onto the front seat with my head down as to avoid any unnecessary contact with the driver and when we come to a stop, I catch my breath and get out of the car.

There is a lot of noise and a lot of action going on in the road behind me. Shit, this is not good. I look at the driver, he isn't moving. Covered in a mixture of blood and milk. I leave him and notice an underpass just a few feet away from us. This is my escape route. I walk away from the wreckage, ignoring the shouts from people who have arrived at the scene.

I'm not sure what road I'm on but there is a road sign that suggests I'm on the A442, 14 miles away from Worcester. That doesn't help.

My head is starting to hurt and I'm feeling sick, I need to sit down. There is a bus stop that has a seat, that'll do nicely thank you very much. The ground is spinning with every step I take. I notice I have milk and blood on my top and from the feel of it, on my face as well.
The bus stop can wait, I need to lay down. I collapse on an embankment and close my eyes.

The motionless ground is spinning, rotating, moving in a way I have never felt it move before. I've been drunk enough times to know what a spinning room feels like but this is different. This is horrible. I need to change my clothes, but I can't right now. I need to just lay here with my eyes closed for a few minutes. I think I'm hidden enough within the unkempt grass and bushes to remain out of sight for the next however long it is. I need to stop doing this...

The nausea and headache have passed, as have a number of emergency vehicles.
I'm at the bus stop now and the gossip suggests that this has become the talk of the town. Rumour has it that it was an older gentleman who lost control of his car and crashed. The tragedy being that he wasn't wearing his seat belt. If he had, then that would have saved his life. That made me smile. There was no mention of a

passenger so that's good.
Now I'm feeling a little better it's time to work out where I am and head back to the station. I'm going back home today as I need some rest. F, G, H, I, J and K have drained me.

To live, love
While the flame is strong,
For we won't be the young ones very long.

SIXTEEN : HATRED

A
AT
ATE
HATE
HATED
HATRED

O (?)
LO (?)
LOE (?)
LOVE
LOVER
LOVERS

Hatred flows with ease. Love is stumbling and guess work. Eventually gets to where you want it to be but then temptation becomes strong and we can't help but share our newfound ability to love with others. Hatred is pure.

I have fallen in and out of love many times yet hate stays.
True hatred is an incredible feeling and one that can lead you to do incredible things. Is it negative? Possibly, but then I've never been hurt by someone because I hated them. Love has left me hurt multiple

times and I know it would do it again and again, if I let it.

Late at night my door knocks as my shadow returns home. With it he brings an overwhelming sense of fear, shame and regret, but it is short-lived. His form scares me. Long thin arms, small body and an enormous head. Colourless yet full of rage. I absorb all the emotions and conflicts held within my shadow and turn to face what I truly hate the most, and that is myself.

I worry sometimes that my skull is shrinking as the skin on my face gets looser. My teeth are also getting smaller. The dentist tells me I have to stop grinding my teeth, but I can't. I've tried to wear a gumshield to bed, but it's just ridiculous and after about 4 minutes I gag so have to spit it out. I also brush my teeth too hard. Whenever I have a new toothbrush, I wear the bristles out within a few days and I never remember to buy a new one. I don't use it every day anyway. There are days I don't wash. Days I don't speak and days when all I want to do is die. My dark days are dark days. I can't create or do anything that brings joy or positivity into my life. I feel empty.

My heart rate is faster than it should be. My breathing is shallow. I experience heart palpitations, anxiety and excessive sweating for no reason. Nothing can calm me, yet it will all suddenly stop, and I'll feel ok. Until it begins again. During these days I can't make eye contact with myself in the mirror. The reflection disgusts me. I'm fatter than I used to be. Older than I used to be. Uglier than I used to be. I convince myself I have a brain tumour or prostate cancer. Every few days I'll go online and check the symptoms of someone with a brain tumour, and I'm sure a load of those apply to me.

Twenty years ago, I suffered a severe concussion when I was embroiled in a mass brawl outside a club. I don't even know who hit me, but I can remember they pinned me against a wall as the police were on the way to restore order, and some asshole walked over to me and punched me right in the face.

As I mentioned, I was being pinned against a wall, so my head had nowhere to go once his fist had made contact. I remember it fucking hurting, but I just smiled back at him, which prompted him to raise his fist once more, just as the flashing blue lights arrived. He never got off that second punch.

I went to my friends place and grabbed myself a hammer. I then headed back to the venue but hid in the stairwell of a block of flats. Waiting for any of those who attacked me an hour earlier. Time passed and no one showed, so I headed back to my friends to get some sleep.

The next day I couldn't walk properly. I kept falling over and whenever I looked to my left, I would feel sick. This led to a trip to the hospital and a severe concussion diagnosis after they found bruising on the brain. I can't

remember much after that, except it took a while to get my balance back to normal. As far as doctor or hospital check-ups, I don't recall any.
This was also all around the time my OCD really kicked in.

OCD, psychosis, borderline personality disorder and bipolar. At one time or another, medical professionals suggested that I may have at least one of those mental disorders.
Throw into that depression and anxiety and you can imagine how difficult it is to be me sometimes. The constant conversations in my head. The rules I have to live by which I don't appear to control over. The constant battles about which socks I can wear and which cutlery I can use.
Here's an example; I have a few different colognes which I use and one of them is Lacoste White which I'd say I have used well over half the bottle but all of a sudden, hang on.

Whilst sharing this story with you I have had to get up and spray some of this on me to counteract the information I'm going to share. First time I've sprayed it on me in quite some time. Smells nice enough. Not the best one I've got, but it's ok. So, the reason I haven't sprayed it for so long is because the bottle itself is pure white. Square in shape but pure white, and that is the same colour as a child's coffin. So, if I use the spray, there will be a death of a child within my family.

Therefore, I can no longer use it. Annoying, yes, but those are the rules. This rule didn't exist when I started using the spray, but it does now, and there are others.

1. I can only wear odd socks.

2. I can't wear socks that have red as a dominant colour.

3. When I've done some washing, the tea towels must dry separately from the other clothes because tea towels are dirty.

4. When emptying the washing machine, if any clothes fall on the floor, they have to go back in the machine to get washed again because I don't know if they are clean or not.

5. When making a cup of tea or coffee, I have to be careful with the milk. I can't mix milk from one bottle with the milk from a different bottle because one cow is responsible for the milk in one bottle and another cow for the milk in the other bottle. Mixing cow juice isn't advised, so I tend to just throw away the last drops of milk from the bottle as to avoid cross contamination.

6. I have to click my fingers on my right hand 3 times when locking a door but just once when locking a window.

7. I can see germs, which means I no longer use a dishwasher because I found I had to wash everything again anyway because there were still germs in the cups and on everything else.

8. Can't drink water from a tap because it's dirty thanks to the metal, rusted pipes and all the rat faeces and tears. Branded bottled mineral water only. Sparkling or still, I'm not fussy.

9. Numbers control so much more than I care to admit. All number combinations I see get added together to make a final single digit number. That single digit number will dictate how good the day or hour will be. 1 is awful, 9 is the best. Can't have 10 because 1 + 0 = 1. So, although we consider 10 to be the top when it comes to scoring things out of 10, I can't have 10 because it's actually 1. The best I can ever hope for is a 9, therefore never being able to experience the perfect day. Because it doesn't exist.

There are plenty more, but it's hard to remember them because half the time I don't know I'm doing anything considered odd until somebody points it out. Plus, it's good that I stop at 9 because as we know, 10 doesn't exist.

Going back to the white cologne / child coffin scenario, and OCD in general, one of my therapists once said to me I don't control the world with my mind, which I understand that, but it will not stop me from repeating this and other rituals or obsessions. Another mental health professional also told me it's just thinking, and they became the best 3 words I had heard in a long, long time. It's just thinking. Of course it is! It's all inside my head. So why can't I control it?

I've been told that these rituals are habits we have learnt and all we have to do is unlearn them, but that in itself is difficult as these rituals are providing relief from anxieties we may have such as, the fear of someone breaking into your home. This could so easily become a problem with excessive or repetitive locking and checking of doors and windows. Over time, this becomes a bigger and bigger issue and will inevitably impact on other areas of your life.
Is the toaster off?
Is my laptop in my bag?
Are the roads safe?
You challenge other people to check that they can cope.

Scenario;

I'm taking the kids out tomorrow.

Where.

Just to the small farm outside of town.

How you getting there?

Driving.

What roads will you be using?

I don't know. The usual route I suppose.

You can't just suppose. Make sure when you go the kids are strapped in. Don't let them hang out the window without a seatbelt on.

When have I ever done that?

Natalia Borodina.

What?

She was hanging out of a window..

Stop. I've taken the kids out plenty of times and there has never been a problem. Today there will not be a problem.

Text me when you get there won't you.

Of course.

Did you want me to come with you? It will be a nice day.

No, you have your appointment at 10 so you need to go to that.

No I don't.

You do otherwise this thing keeps going on and on and on.

What thing?

This! This sudden fear of me driving with the kids.

I just worry.

No. This goes beyond worry which is why you need to go to this appointment this morning. It is all in your head. Nothing is going to happen. Nothing happened last time and nothing will happen this time.

You sure?

Yes, I'm sure.

These types of conversations are dangerous. Asking if the door is locked once, can easily lead to asking if the door is locked again, and again. This simple question can grow and grow into asking if the door and windows are locked. Is the toaster unplugged? The oven off? Leaving the house becomes more and more difficult as the checks become more and more time-consuming.

Are all the lights off? Are all the light switches facing the correct way? Are the plugs the correct distance away from the sockets?

It's not just your emotional state that gets damaged with this forced anxiety, but also that of your loved ones. They can see it. They hear it. They live it.
You force your anxieties onto them and in time they resent you and will walk away. I never wanted her to walk away but she did. I forced Dani away from me. I did it. It's my fault.

Long gone are the days when OCD was considered the quirky one of all the mental disorders when all you do is clean and put your DVDs in alphabetical order.

I have OCD.
Ooh, your house must be lovely and clean!

No, it isn't. Another thing OCD isn't - an adjective. Fastidious. Use that word instead of using OCD. Being tidy or attentive to detail does not mean you have OCD. If someone asks you when you were diagnosed, do not take offence. You were never diagnosed because you do not have Obsessive Compulsive Disorder. You just like to tidy stuff.

OCD goes beyond the finger clicking, light switch flicking and door locking / unlocking physical rituals because not everything with OCD is visible. Purely Obsessional, otherwise known as Pure O, is OCD but the sufferer engages in hidden compulsions. Intrusive thoughts and mental rituals create a mind that is overcrowded and under constant pressure.

I have Pure O.

SEVENTEEN : LEEDS

Have you ever lived on, or spent any time on a council estate? Maybe you once visited someone who, perhaps, lived on the eighth floor of a tower block? Tenth floor? Fourteenth floor? Or maybe you've driven past a council estate or seen one on TV? On the news perhaps when they talk about the poorest people who inhabit the UK. Or perhaps when the media needs to show an area of deprivation and desperation. Do you know the areas I'm on about?

I spent many, many years of my life on these estates and yeah, I have witnessed and been a victim of some nasty events. I've been mugged, beaten up, hospitalised (couple of times), listened to armed police raids on a neighbour's flat after a fatal shooting. At Christmas time, I've seen parents searching through the communal bins for old discarded toys to give to their own kids as Christmas gifts. I learnt about suicide, underage sex and drugs.

I've watched men kerb crawling and picking up young women, but one thing I never saw, or heard in all the years of living in these places was a climate change protest. Or people blockading a budget frozen supermarket or the local shop shouting 'Meat Is Murder'.

There were no safe spaces or cry closets and facts came before feelings.

Some of the people that lived in these places were utter cunts, but at least they were honest. You knew your place, and everyone just got on with it. I made some really strong friendships, and we all grew up together in the concrete jungle. We fought together, fought against each other, drank wine and smoked weed. Fumbled in the bushes, rumbled in the parks and only went home when it got dark.

The only protest I ever remember happening were the ones against the Poll Tax in the early 1990s and that anger was targeted at the government. Never did I see a protest for black-trans rights or the gender pay gap. Next time you get into a conversation with someone about veganism or some crap like that, just ask them about those who live in poverty. Those who live payday to payday. Those who live in a concrete container with 100 other people living above and below them. Do those people give a shit about your tedious rhetoric or middle class agendas. No, of course not, because when it all boils down to it, all we want to do is survive. The rest is social media point scoring. Who can be the most hard done by, the most offended, the most triggered. Council estate *scum* are 100% better than **you** sanctimonious bags of pretentious shit.

I'm in a cafe sipping on an iced mocha and there are two bitches sat in front of me who fit the above description perfectly. They are the type of girls that go to summer festivals, paint unicorns on their faces and enjoy overpriced dried out vegan turd burgers even though the land on which they dance is a dairy farm. They strive to outlaw clapping as is may trigger someone with high anxiety issues. Instead, they resort to waving jazz hands about. Sadly, because of their ambitions, the blind will never know what is going on. That's discrimination, isn't it?

One of girls gets up to leave and does that stupid air kiss thing near her friends' cheek and blurts out 'chao babes' before leaving. Chao babes! We're in fucking Leeds. A few minutes later and blondie is on the move. I need to finish my drink and follow.

Within two minutes we have arrived at a hotel. Does she work here or is she staying here? That was a really short walk, shame really because she had a beautiful arse. I could have walked behind her for miles, but for now I'll have to make do with just standing behind her in the queue at the check-in desk. She smells amazing.

Hi, I'm checking in.

Ok, thank you. What was the name?

Saskia Lloyd. I'm staying for 2 nights.

Ah yes thank you. It is all sorted for you Miss Lloyd and you are in room 26.

At this point I turn away and pretend to answer a call on my mobile. She is in room 26 but first I need to sort myself out. I've counted multiple cameras between the cafe and the hotel lobby and I have to assume that every one of them has clocked me. I walk over to the bar and order a large whisky, with what I can only describe as a Mexican voice? I really must stop doing these. This one was on the verge of sounding like that mouse, Speedy Gonzales. I make polite and light conversation with the barman, finish my drink and leave.

I need the toilet. I've had two coffees and a large whisky since arriving in Leeds and now I need a piss. I need to get my head back in the game, but, and there is always a but, I'm here again. I am back again at this place I've never been, again! Yet the déjà vu is so overwhelming. I walk out onto Park Place and there, at the end of the road is the building I have seen so many times before. In memories or dreams, I don't know, but I certainly recognise it. My heart skips a beat and I feel breathless, anxious. Does this building follow me around?
Of course not, buildings don't have legs. But chairs have legs. Clocks have hands. Your bed has a foot. Combs have teeth and roads have shoulders. So maybe buildings can move around?

An empty black hearse drives past me. It's empty because it's waiting for me. The building is following me around and now as I'm drawing nearer to the end of my journey the hearse is waiting for me. The driver looks at me and smiles; I think. He knows the end is coming. He knows that I'm on borrowed time and he knows my name. How does he know my name?

The number plate, **KA26 ABV**. I don't know what the ABV means but KA are my initials, and the festival bitch is in room 26.
ABV. Abhorrent bloody violence? A black vehicle?
Why has someone wearing red just walked past me?
Red = dead. In the Mr. Men books Mr. Strong is red and he gets hit by a bus.

The number 18 bus goes by. 1 + 8 = 9 and 9 is a good number, as long as I don't see two more. Another bus passes the opposite way. The number 27.
2 + 7 = 9.
9 + 9 = 18.
1 + 8 = 9.

Why does every multiple of 9 add up to 9?
5 x 9 = 45. 4 + 5 = 9.
17 x 9 = 153. 1 + 5 + 3 = 9.
241 x 9 = 2169. 2 + 1 + 6 + 9 = 18. 1 + 8 = 9.
3507 x 9 = 31563. 3 + 1 + 5 + 6 + 3 = 18. 1 + 8 = 9.
70664 x 9 = 635976. 6 + 3 + 5 + 9 + 7 + 6 = 36. 3 + 6 = 9.

Try it. No matter what number you multiply by 9, it's going to add up to 9.

Once again, my mind has wandered, and all this has happened in the space of a few seconds, and now I feel confused. Why do I always have these episodes of paranoia and fear? I remind myself that I am fear. I control paranoia and fear. I am not at the end of my journey, I'm not even halfway. I am in Leeds not Yarmouth, so have plenty more kills to go. I need to get my head back in the zone. Fuck the building and fuck the hearse. I've got a job to do so head on down King Street, turn another corner and end up back at the café where I started, which is good because they have a toilet.

Five minutes later and I am on my way back to the hotel. I just hope Miss Lloyd is still there and not gone out. I'm not sure how much time has passed since I left her at the check-in desk. Twenty minutes? An hour? I have no idea.

I walk into the hotel, say hello to the girl at the desk and head for the stairs. On my way up to the first floor, I have to admit that this is a really striking building both inside and out. Got to be a Grade 2 listed building or something along those lines. I wonder what a building like this is worth? Why don't they make new hotels look like these old style buildings instead of just going with the same generic box design with rooms that are pretty much just portacabins stacked on top of one another? Anyway, where am I going? Room 26, here we are. Let's knock and see what happens.

Saskia is so beautiful. She believed me when I said that I am a guest at the hotel and there has been a double booking. I am supposed to be in room 26.
She is so very beautiful. Long, soft blonde hair, strong yet subtle features. Lips so full and perfect that with even the softest of kisses she would render a man helpless. She is wearing a floral skirt with a cropped floral top. She has perfectly sculptured curves and her voice; her voice is so soft. I could listen to her speaking to me all day.

It's a real shame I have to kill her, but she made a fundamental error. She invited me into her room.

Are you sure you're in room 26?

Yeah, I've just arrived, and reception said the room had been double booked. The problem is my pregnant wife is due at the hotel in a couple of hours and I really don't want to have to muck her about.

Oh no I totally get that.

Do you have your room details?

Sure, come in and I'll find them. I'm happy to change rooms if that would be easier for you?

If you could that would be amazing. My name is Mick.

Hi Mick, I'm Saskia.

Those were her final words.

As she walked away from me and toward the desk in her room, I moved quickly behind her. I plunged my knife into her neck as hard as I could. The blade went from underneath her jaw down to her collarbone. She didn't make any noise. Not even a whimper.
She fell to her knees, pointlessly holding her open wound as tightly as she could, knowing it would do nothing to prevent the inevitable. Her life was over.
I was about to insert my blade into her throat once again when I caught my reflection in the mirror. I had an erection. I had a fucking erection!

Saskia, you truly are beautiful.
Her pale face was just inches from my penis, and I desperately wanted her to consume me. I wanted to face fuck her but didn't think that was appropriate for a first date. Instead, I knelt beside her and gently cupped her breasts. The light in her eyes was fading, yet she tried so hard not to die. I wanted her to know I was aroused, so I pulled her top down to expose her young, firm breasts and continued to caress them. We stared at each other. She was gasping for the final time as I was massaging her, using her blood as an essential oil. We made eye contact one last time as she stared at me in a

way I've not seen in a long time. I think it was love. I think we're in love. I moved closer to her and gently kissed her perfect mouth, then slowly lowered her body onto the floor as I lay down beside her.

A few hours have passed since Saskia said goodbye to the world yet I'm still here in room 26, and yes, she is still beautiful. And no, I haven't fucked her, but I did explore her. What I mean is, I stripped her naked and indulged in every inch of her body. From her toes to her hair. I touched, kissed and cradled her, making sure she knew she was being looked after and cared for. Her legs, so plain yet toned without a hint of fatty deposits. Silky smooth. My fingers move slowly, retracing the places others have been before. Her vagina, clean and inviting. I wanted to take a closer look, but as I've already said, for a first date this was a little too much, too soon.

Milky white skin covered her internal organs. Her stomach, so flat and her waist so narrow. I moved my attention up to her ribs and with my fingers pushed as hard as I could below the cage where her heart is. I want it. I want her. I miss her already.

Why did she have to walk away from me. Turning her back and leave the way she did. She could not see me cry, begging for her return. Please, tell me why. I deserve to know why. Why did you leave me.

Saskia has a fragrance that is so sensual. Notes of soft vanilla push me to taste her so I can remember her.

Absorb her scent so I can find her once again in the most unexpected of places. But now, it is time say goodbye.

I put her naked body into bed and covered her with the duvet. Hopefully she'll have a pleasant sleep, she deserves it. Such a shame she is dead. So beautiful.
I need to go, my train leaves soon, but first I need to set fire to the room. Burning down the room was the straightforward part, saying goodbye to Saskia, not so straightforward. I pour all the flammable liquid I can find in her room all over the bed and set it alight. As I walk away the fire alarms go off and panic spreads throughout the hotel. I am now just another person in the crowd trying to get out.

I'm on the train and heading toward Manchester, I'm staying there tonight. Should be back by 10pm at the latest. I have a few beers and food waiting for me and a big comfortable bed which I cannot wait to climb into, but first I need some female company. A couple hundred quid will get me what I need for tonight. I want a blonde and she will be called Saskia.

Saskia.
There was no rain my love, so forever you will burn.

EIGHTEEN : MACCLESFIELD

In the next few months I've got it in my head I've got to kill somebody.
It could be the Shard, it could be anything just as long as it's a high thing and we can go up and visit it and then push somebody off it and I know for a fact they'll die from falling from a hundred feet.

Not my words but those (allegedly) of a young man who (allegedly) told his carers what he was going to do, and then in August 2019 he attempted to do just that. The incident made headline news and raised questions around the care he received.

I remember sitting in one of my therapy sessions and talking about one particular evening from my past when I roamed the streets carrying a knife with the sole intent of killing someone. I even went into detail about how I watched a young woman walk past me, on her own, wearing a light coloured jacket, short blonde hair and even shorter skirt. I hid behind a wall as she glided past me in slow motion. I imagined sinking my blade deep into her neck and draining the life from her in the piss stained shadows of a nearby alleyway. She kept on walking as I continued to stare. The moment had passed, and I didn't attack her. I let her continue her journey along this road, and I do not know if I've ever seen her since. Maybe I have? Imagine that. We could have been standing side by side in a supermarket as two strangers doing nothing more than exchanging pleasantries as we wait for our turn to buy our toilet rolls and bread. We could have been standing together waiting for the same bus. We could also have been part of the same news report. A story in the local and no doubt national press that would have linked us together forever. Hunter, prey. Unnecessary death. Random attack. But it didn't happen. I let you walk.

I refused to go home, so I walked across the road to the car park and slashed the tyres on as many cars as I could before panic set in.

I think I slashed the tyres of at least 20 cars. I say slashed, but it was more of a stab. Pushing the blade into the tyre once or twice in the hope they would deflate. I didn't stay long enough to find out, but they did all make a hissing noise when penetrated. As soon as I stabbed one, I moved onto the next.

The following morning delivered something quite unexpected. I felt conflicted, embarrassed, almost ashamed by what I'd done. A part of me wanted to see what chaos I had created but then I became worried that someone would, somehow know it was me and I would be publicly named and shamed as this sad, pathetic man who punctured tyres for some unknown reason and now has to pay the bill to repair them all. So with that in mind, I went with the safe option and stayed at home, for about three days.

The lack of concern and interest shared by the therapist when I disclosed the information about wanting to kill, made me feel that my desires were nothing more than standard behaviour. Fantasy talk. I don't think she realised I was telling the truth and concluded that there was nothing to be worried about so yet again, I walked away from the session confused and thinking this kind of support was not for me. I say support but what I mean is, this box ticking exercise of going through the motions in a sterile room with an equally sterile individual asking the same formulated questions that she has many times before me, and will ask again with those who follow.

I keep reminding myself that we are not patients, we are numbers. We are not patients, we are numbers. A part of a future infographic that goes no way in explaining anything. A statistic to make people talk, to make people care for a short while. Not for too long because there is other stuff happening, and we have such busy lives you know. Lives in which we are too busy to stop and take stock of what is happening. Our physical and mental health deteriorates so we turn to those little white pills to help us balance out the chemical imbalance in our heads, but what about the imbalance in our lives?

I don't have the answers, most of the time I don't even understand the question, yet we are all here today because we survived. Nothing more than that, we just survived. There is no higher power, no reincarnation, no afterlife, and one day someone will say your name for the last time.

Tomorrow the world will keep on turning, and again the next day. Turning, spinning, doing what it's done for billions of years. We scrap, fight and kill to make it through to tomorrow, but for what? To grow old and have My Way played at our funeral. You never did it your way, you are all controlled. We are all controlled. Controlled and manipulated by a higher power, even though it doesn't exist. So, what is the answer? As I said, I don't even understand the question.

I am suddenly and rudely interrupted, as this prayer meeting comes to an end. I'm sat in a church in Macclesfield, it's early evening and I have just spent an hour in the company of some of the wettest people I have ever met. Without regret I could have slaughtered every single one of them and I don't think society would have missed them, except perhaps on those summer fate days when Janet judges the jam competition. But I refrained from such activities as I'm staying here for a couple of nights at a hotel which is just a couple of minutes away from the station. That's why I ended up here at this prayer meeting, I mean, I have time to kill (pun intended) before I have to leave and head back home.

As I was about to head out the door, one of the slightly more attractive ladies in attendance touched me gently

on the arm and mentioned that she and a few of the others will be off to the pub now as its become a bit of a tradition and I am welcome to tag along.
The pub isn't far, so I can see why it's a weekly tradition. Have a nice prayer meeting followed by wine and crisps at the local. I order the drinks as a token of my appreciation for being accepted into the group and sit down at the table. Once we had got past the awkward questions like who are you? and what made you come to the prayer meeting? The conversation was enjoyable and free flowing. Around an hour or so has passed and I must admit that I'm actually enjoying myself. A few people have gone, but there are still a few of us left. Just thinking about it, this is the first time I have socially interacted with other people in, I have no idea in how long? Months probably.

It's now coming up to 10pm, and it's just me and my new friend Milena left to finish our drinks. She then asks me a question to which the answer can only be yes.

Can you walk me home?

She doesn't live too far, and it's all downhill, so not a tough walk.
As we walked together along the dark and quiet streets of Macclesfield, she asked the obvious next questions, are you married, do you have a girlfriend? To which I replied, no. Which is true and I think the only true thing I said all evening. I lied about my name, my job and my

reasons for being north of London. We get to her door and rather than ask if I want to come in, she just kisses me. We kiss again, and this time for longer. This is not the plan. This is not the fucking plan, yet I can't take my hands off of her. We fall onto her floor as the door slams shut behind us. In what feels like just a few seconds I am inside her. She is hot, wet and riding me hard.

Have you ever killed someone?

What.

Have you ever killed someone?

What are you talking about?

Since Andover I have followed you across the country and I knew that when you got to the letter M you would find me.

I try to push her off of me, but I can't. This is agony and ecstasy all rolled into one. She grinds harder and faster, leans forward and puts her hand around my throat.

Now it's my turn. I was the toilet attendant in that restaurant, and I saw what you did to that poor boy. You horrible little cunt.

What the fuck are you talking about?

I call this payback. Time to catch up once again with Hammerhead.

Get off me. GET THE FUCK OFF OF ME!

Everyone in the prayer room is staring at me. I am totally breathless, totally confused, and still they stare. I have to go.

The journey back to the hotel was a blur. I do not know what is going on.

I check the time, it is 6:06pm. I'm in my room now so I can just relax, sit and take stock of everything that just happened, but nothing happened. Nothing happened! I sat in that fucking church and went mental. I strip off and lay out on my bed. Breathe.

6. 6. 6.

I check the time as I think I fell asleep. It's 3:20am. Fuck, I did fall asleep and now I'm awake stupid early. I run myself a bath and have a long soak. I feel ok now; I leave Macclesfield tomorrow, so I need to get the kill done today.

It's just gone 7am so I head off and my plan is to just walk and eventually something will happen that I can take advantage of. Terrible plan I know, but it’s all I’ve got.

I’ve been out for a few hours now. Got myself some breakfast, had a coffee and had a pleasant chat with some crazy old woman who was shouting at the birds for some reason or another, and now I’m walking along The Silk Road. Wasn’t that a marketplace on the dark web once upon a time?
Hang on, am I still asleep. What is with this town?
The freak out last night and now I’m walking on an illegal website.
Maybe that crazy old woman wasn’t crazy after all?
Maybe she had something to tell me and I couldn’t understand her because I was listening to the wrong words.

I stop walking and argue with myself about going back or not. Fuck it, I need to see if I can find her and see what she knows.

It’s now early afternoon and I’m back on The Silk Road. I couldn’t find the crazy old woman, so I guess the birds had heard enough, clubbed together and flew off with her. At this moment they are probably pecking away at her old saggy skin as she shouts at them repeatedly. The birds can hear her noise, but they don’t care because they will remove her tongue soon. They have already removed her eyes.

With the sharp of the beak they penetrated the whites of her eyes and follow the path to the internal juicy parts of her head. Once the eyes had been removed, tiny birds like the sparrows, tits and finches, journey into the hole and get to work on removing the brain. All this time the crazy lady moans and whimpers, wishing she had never started on those birds to begin with.

I rest against a graffiti-covered wall and stare into the road. The world I create in my head is so much more than the world I was born into. When I sleep, I rule. I know this place in my head and I feel safe there. Once again, I ask myself the question, why don't you just kill yourself right now? I ask this of me way more than I probably should. I could do it now and if I leave the M page in my pocket and it would just look like I was victim thirteen and his legend will live on because they will never...

Hey guy, wanna buy some weed? Wanna buy some weed?

Huh.

You're standing about on the Silk Road. What you want?

Erm weed yeah, or maybe something a little stronger.

Ah is it. Come with me. Follow.

What is it with people wanting to keep selling me weed?
As instructed, I follow this thing off of The Silk Road and behind some kind of empty looking builders shed overgrown with bushes and; I get it now. I can see two more of these urban foot soldiers over in the corner. Hoods up and talking to each other in some kind of feral street language?

Guy, my boy wants to know how much you got.

Got? What do you mean, got?

Money. What you got?

Money, right. On me I have £400 but I can get more.

Why you carrying that much money around. There are a lot of bad people around here that will take that from you and cut you up.

Really? I've never had trouble before.

Another one of the feral children joins in with the conversation.

Shut up bruv, I ain't seen you round here before.

Yeah because I've never had to buy from this far up before but my boys in Stafford, well let's just say things have dried up so I'm looking for pastures new.

This is bullshit. Look at you.

Look at me, what?

You ain't no roadman or dealer. Shit, you ain't even a user. You just a basic bitch and now we called you out.

Ok, ok I'm sorry. Yes, I am lying but that was just to buy time so I could see what I was up against, men or boys.

You got some cheek. Coming down here, lying to me and then saying this shit about us being men or boys.

Look, would it help if I went and got us all chicken?

Fuck you. See this blade, I'm going to cut your throat. Now give me that coin.

It's in my back pocket. In my wallet, take it. I'm sorry, I'm nervous, scared.

One of the twats walks around the back of me and pulls my wallet out whilst his shit ugly friend keeps glaring at me and waving his knife in my face.

As I stare deep into the black of his eyes something within me clicks. It's like everything has suddenly just fallen into place and I know who I am. The weight I've

been carrying around in my mind has gone. My head feels light, but not in a way where I feel dizzy or sick.
I feel amazing. I can feel a tingle running down my spine and across my skin. I have goosebumps. I get it and my purpose is clear.
I am ready to change the lives of these filthy, feral bastards and deliver a moment of clarity they will never forget.
The twat behind me opens my wallet and lets out a shriek of excitement.

The boy ain't lying! There's got to be £400 in here like he said. Gav, go get the boys, we having a party.

Twat number 3 runs off which gives me enough of a distraction to bring out my own knife, except this is one of my favourite OTF knives and although the blade is only two inches, that's all I need.
Before anyone can react, shit ugly falls to his knees as I sink my blade deep into his eye socket. He took all my two inches and didn't even flinch. I turn my attentions to the coward with my wallet.

Sorry man, we just playing. Have your wallet back.

What's his name?

Who?

The cunt with my knife stuck in his fucking head. What's his name?

Kendall.

I can see honest terror in his eyes and for the first time since I've been in this weird town, I feel alive. A smile creeps across my face as I remove a second knife from my sleeve and plunge it into the other eye socket of the boy Kendall. I push his body to the floor and turn my attention back to the wallet holder.

Who are you?

Don't hurt me man, seriously, I have a little girl and a mum.

Who are you?

My name. My name is Raj.

Ok Raj, take my money and buy something for your kid and start your life again.

What do you mean?

Take the money and run. Run as far away from this life as you can.

Thank you, thank you.

I want you to take this as well.

What is it?

It's a piece of paper. When the Police come knocking at your door, and they will, I want you to give this to them and tell them it's from me.

Ok yeah, yeah I will, but who are you?

My name is Kane Azika. I am Alpha, the black vulture. Now fuck off!

With that, I feel like I have truly arrived. Alpha, the Black Vulture. I like the name and like what I've just done. I feel amazing, the best I have felt in a long, long time. My skin is tingling and the hairs on my arms are standing.

ABV. Alpha Black Vulture. The hearse in Leeds! The fucking hearse had the number plate: **KA26 ABV**. Kane Azika. 26 letters of the alphabet, 26 kills as Alpha, the Black Vulture.
The bringer of death.
So, it is all true. I am more than just a number, a tick in a box, a forgettable statistic on an infographic. I am the game changer. The one that is going to make people sit up and take notice. This isn't about mental illness, I'm

better now. This is about revenge and my god am I hungry.

I look back at Kendall. The sack of shit is dead and much like the old crazy woman, his eyes have been destroyed.

Wherever you believe your spirit, or your soul moves onto next, the eyes will be of no use to you.
You are forever damned to be in darkness.

I remove the blades from his eyes and slam them with full force, simultaneously into his ears.
You are forever damned to be in silence.

I take one more knife from my pocket and open his mouth. I pause for a few seconds as I can feel anger and hatred flow through my veins.
This is so you may never speak my name.

I force my knife so hard into his throat that I dislocate his jaw. I stand above him, triumphant. His blood-stained face morphs into the portraits of all those who have crossed me and all those who have yet to try.

I feel as though I have removed the fear from my life. I feel liberated. I feel powerful. As I walk away from this carnage, I turn back onto The Silk Road and head toward the hotel.

Its a very warm day, the sun is bright, yet I cast no shadow.
Maybe, I am finally alone.

PART ONE OF A THREE PART SERIES

ALPHA : ONE
RISE OF THE BLACK VULTURE

ALPHA : TWO
TWO SIDES TO EVERY STORY

ALPHA : THREE
KILLING YOU IS NOT ENOUGH

www.isolacium.co.uk

Printed in Great Britain
by Amazon

30200787R00119